# Accelerate the Metaverse
## David Caiati

Published by Karmic Robot, LLC

Copyright © 2024 by David Caiati

First Edition


All rights reserved.

No portion of this book may be reproduced in any form

without written permission from David Caiati

or Karmic Robot LLC,

except as permitted by U.S. copyright law.


www.karmicrobot.com


This is a work of fiction.

Any resemblance of any persons or AIs,

living or dead, is purely coincidental.


ISBN 979-8-9909282-3-7

This book is dedicated to
all who try to make the world
a better place.
A world filled with love,
tolerance, and respect.
A world without hatred or killer AIs.

# Contents

1. Sausage Position — 1
2. Travails — 5
3. The Metaverse — 8
4. A Rose by Any Other Name — 12
5. Fish Tales — 17
6. More People-y — 21
7. Feeding the Masses — 25
8. Turkey Club, Extra Mayo, Extra Bacon, No Lettuce — 28
9. A Life — 32
10. An Artificial Life — 37
11. Solitude — 41
12. Intelligence — 46
13. Sindy — 50
14. We Talked About This — 54
15. Robert — 58
16. Lunch on Main St — 61

| | | |
|---|---|---|
| 17. | Willow | 65 |
| 18. | Justin | 68 |
| 19. | The Point Is | 71 |
| 20. | Serenity Dissolved | 75 |
| 21. | Show Time | 79 |
| 22. | Pre-Launch | 82 |
| 23. | Ultrix Blows Up | 85 |
| 24. | Secret Places | 88 |
| 25. | An Accident | 93 |
| 26. | Sabotage? | 99 |
| 27. | New Dave (Meets an AI) | 102 |
| 28. | Ashore | 106 |
| 29. | Roger in the Sandbox | 109 |
| 30. | Campfire | 112 |
| 31. | IRL | 116 |
| 32. | A Few Drinks | 120 |
| 33. | A Chance Encounter | 123 |
| 34. | More Friends | 127 |
| 35. | Walter Eight | 130 |
| 36. | Walter Arrives | 134 |
| 37. | Walter Dies | 136 |
| 38. | Now You See Her | 139 |

| | | |
|---|---|---|
| 39. | The Unseen | 142 |
| 40. | A Day at the Beach | 145 |
| 41. | Can't Wait | 148 |
| 42. | Dave and Walter | 151 |
| 43. | What a Dick | 154 |
| 44. | Another Dick | 157 |
| 45. | A Bag of Dicks | 160 |
| 46. | The Team | 163 |
| 47. | The White Room | 166 |
| 48. | IRL, Again | 169 |
| 49. | Ultrix Two | 172 |
| 50. | Accelerate the Metaverse | 174 |
| 51. | Ultrix Two Goes Online | 178 |
| 52. | Acknowledgements | 180 |
| 53. | Thank You | 181 |

# Sausage Position

Dumpin Crawford did not set out to create a serial killer. The fabrication of a murderous entity was not his goal. He was a kind, intelligent, simple man who aimed toward the higher, more noble endeavor of establishing a perfect society. Dumpin wanted to create a digital paradise, a safe space for humanity, free of the fine detritus of fear and hatred that permeated society in the early 21st century. He aspired to build an online, virtual community that encouraged tolerance, respect, and positivity. In short, a world that he craved to live in.

Alas, forging a utopia was complicated. While Dumpin invested many years of careful, researched, and intentional labor, his efforts inadvertently produced an environment where a psychopathic killer, unlike any in human history, could emerge and develop unchecked until it was too late.

In retrospect, what else could come from a man named *Dumpin*?

All software developers, the good ones anyway, while often suffering from a deep imposter syndrome, have some sort of God complex. They have to. Most of the time, constructing a computer program is not life-or-death like brain surgery or fighting fires. Yet the people who write code can devote their entire day to the creation of something out of nothing, a working thing from a blank editor screen. It's long days of invention and revision until static commands, linked in a proper sequence, produce activity: a robot hand lifts its finger, a digital assistant reports on the weather, or an artificially intelligent algorithm optimizes a routine that leads to murder.

After one of these long days, an important day, the day Dumpin completed the last few lines of code that evolved into the lethal AI, he rested. Slumped, splayed out on a dark green wool couch, surrounded by empty beer bottles, his eyes were gently closed. Two 60-inch LED television screens took up most of the opposite wall in the attic apartment he loosely rented from his uncle, Wilson, a retired fisherman.

A young, bright-eyed doctor or a too-smiling, head-nodding nutritionist or a spirited, indefatigable gym trainer might have said Dumpin was slightly more than *marginally obese*. The term reflected the reality that, in the 2020s in America on Planet Earth, several millennia after some of the most advanced societies (utopias, none of them) had flourished and disappeared, no one knew what the hell they were talking about. And, in fact, many people in his not-quite-quaint ancient fishing community of Arcadia, Massachusetts, considered Dumpin attractively healthy and fortunately big-boned. Actually, most people he passed on Main Street below his apartment window might have even said that he could probably benefit from eating a little more, a little more of *their* home cooking.

Privately, when Dumpin looked down at his stomach flopping over his sweatpants, he acknowledged he had recently gained weight. Without wanting to give the hairy roll much credence, he considered the expanse of skin, when he considered it, a temporary minor nuisance. He maintained that the girth would easily disappear as soon as he returned to a daily jog along the harbor. It was an activity he enjoyed in his forties until he tore his meniscus. The injury gave him the opportunity to embrace the excuse of replacing his energetic run with a slow limp to the local bakery for a bagel and a cup of coffee. After the surgery and his complete recovery, he promised himself he'd get back to it. At 56, with little notice of the time that had passed, his newfound thickness had become as reluctantly stubborn as his general outlook toward self-improvement.

*Reluctantly stubborn.*

No one is purposefully stubborn, right? Dumpin, for sure, was not purposefully stubborn. His disposition simply resulted from the settling into a life of quiet anticipation. A waiting, like most people in the turbulent rush of the twenty-first century, for his turn. Waiting for his chance at the checkout counter at the local liquor store, his pause at the stop sign at the end of Main Street, his opportunity for his fair share in life. Over time, the waiting became the thing itself. His youthful aspirations quietly morphed into a nebulous haze of tomorrows that resembled todays. Routines with no surprises. Not that he was looking for surprises. In software development, surprises usually meant that something had gone wrong.

At 12:11 am, both televisions had found their way to the same channel. He muted the one that was still making noise, rolled around on the couch to position his back toward the glowing monitors, and squeezed his knees up to assume a fetal position. His butt teetered on the edge of the center cushion. His t-shirt rode up his back, exposing the beginnings of a gluteal crevice. He slipped his hands into the warm spot between his knees, wiggled his body to a cozy snuggle, momentarily tensed, and relaxed deeper into the couch's embrace. Within a minute, Dumpin's slow breaths turned into great chainsaw snores as he dreamed of donuts and women's breasts.

He had completed the advanced artificial intelligent template for the beings who were going to inhabit the perfect digital society he was building, the Ultrix metaverse. Creating Ultrix was his job at the Better Worlds Corporation. Dumpin was the sole programmer at the VC-funded company, still in stealth-mode. He might have considered Ultrix his life's work if he had cared enough for things like career and a life's calling. But he didn't. He came to view the project as simply another activity in a long line of programming assignments spread out across a dull and unremarkable career. In the end, for Dumpin, completing the template meant he could move on to other parts of the Better Worlds' metaverse—the building *a utopia* part.

He slept deeply—more deeply, possibly, than he would sleep in the days or years ahead. Dumpin slept so well because he did not know what he had set into motion earlier. He dozed, ignorant of the impending events, of the knowledge that the day would come to represent such a fateful juncture in human history.

He was oblivious to the fact that his AI template, after a few random mutations, would give birth to a relentless and inhumane killer.

# Travails

When Dumpin awoke the next morning, he stood, pulled up his pants, and stretched his arms straight up into the air until his fingers brushed the attic apartment's sloping ceiling. He lifted his heels and rocked on to his toes to press his palms flat into the antique horsehair plaster. A small twinge of pain emerged from his lower back and then eased as he stretched through it. He couldn't remember if the ache was new or not. Or if he needed to stop sleeping on the couch. Either way, he leaned into his flexing and let the ache subside.

Satisfied that he hadn't shrunk overnight, he released his stretch and slumped back down, dropping his arms to his sides. He scanned his apartment for empty beer bottles and dirty dishes, collected as many items as he could carry, and headed downstairs to his uncle's apartment, as was his routine every morning.

He found Wilson sitting at the kitchen table drinking coffee from a chipped mug that declared *World's Best Auntie*. The local newspaper sat in front of him, folded, wrapped in a blue elastic, waiting for anyone to show interest. When Wilson saw Dumpin, he shifted to rise from his chair, as he had done for the last fifty-something years, to make the boy breakfast. Dumpin put a gentle hand on his uncle's shoulder to stop him, as he had done for the last thirty-something years. Wilson looked up at his nephew, smiled, and eased back into his chair. It was their ritual—mechanical and performed every day with as much love as it had the first time it was executed.

Dumpin refilled his uncle's coffee from an old automatic drip machine on the counter, and then he poured himself some into his usual cup: *World's Best Grandma*.

"What's the news?" Dumpin said.

It was a private joke between them. Wilson never read the paper. He just hadn't got around to cancelling the daily subscription. He found out all he needed to know from a nine-seat breakfast and lunch cafe a block from their home called *The Sole Scrod*. Regardless of who was there or when he arrived, Wilson could easily strike up an amicable conversation with anyone. Often, a single topic would engage all the patrons and even include the cook and the cook's wife. The two, Phil and Wanda Spencer, had owned the place for decades, and it remained a beacon for people who made their living off the sea and served as a vital location for the dissemination of Arcadia buzz, important or scandalous or both.

Once Wilson left for his daily communal excursion, Dumpin started a second pot of coffee. While he waited for it to finish brewing, he sat back down at the kitchen table, flopped the newspaper open, and scanned its pages for anything to catch his interest. Eventually, he stopped at the last section. There he scanned the comics, knocked out the puzzles—crossword, Sudoku, and word jumble, and tossed the paper into the recycling bin by the door. The ritual gave order to his day.

Back in the attic with a hot cup of coffee, Dumpin sat at his desk in the corner of the one-room apartment. He considered the space more than a corner. It was his office. His work area was anchored to his desk, but his work space spilled into most of the room. When he sat to work, Dumpin was surrounded by computer equipment, books shelves, file cabinets, and white boards—it was a modern, technological command center, the hub of his existence.

The aesthetic of his work arena was at odds with the colonial chamber within which it resided. The apartment was ancient, having been finished as a bedroom almost a century earlier. It was drafty and smelled of time and human occupation. In the winter, the only heat emanated from Dumpin's computer equipment, which was constantly running. In warmer weather, unscreened open windows, an oscillating fan, and a strong sea breeze off the harbor afforded him his only means of cooling.

It was 9:30 in the morning on a warm spring day, and the fan was blasting lukewarm salt air into this cocoon of technology. Dumpin Crawford didn't notice the temperature or the fluctuating air fluttering papers scattered at his feet. He put his virtual reality goggles on his head, shifting the lenses over his eyeglasses, and entered Ultrix—the sterile, digital, perfect universe he was creating. It was time to get to work.

# The Metaverse

Dumpin stood alone in the middle of a wide avenue in the heart of an enormous digital city. The air was still. In fact, there was no air, no breeze. There was no sound. He hadn't turned it on. Dumpin liked the silence. He didn't want it to distract from his inspection of the visuals detail.

The buildings on either side of him were in ultra-high resolution, clean, distinct, perfectly scaled. As he scanned the street in all directions, his surroundings stretched and faded and became less defined, pixelated. It was all intentional. The effects of living in a computer-generated world. And, it was performing perfectly as he imagined it—the player saw what was up close and didn't waste effort focusing on objects that were too far away. It was efficient, and his algorithm was functioning ideally.

In the middle of a wide avenue, Dumpin stood, looking around, inspecting every angle. To another user, his player avatar appeared as a middle-aged woman dressed in a safari outfit, khaki pants and shirt, black boots, and long, flowing red hair pouring out from beneath an Indiana Jones' fedora. While there were many adornments available in the Ultrix metaverse, such as belts, scarfs, jewelry, capes, and pets, Dumpin kept his personification understated, except for the hat.

He wandered around Ultrix to perform a final quality control assessment before sharing the most recent incarnation with his boss, his boss's boss, and a room full of C-level executives—the administrative chieftains of the Better Worlds Corporation. Dumpin was pleased with what he saw. His metaverse only marginally exceeded the expectation he had set at the previous product review. He anticipated it would allow him to keep their confidence and buy him the liberty to continue to work relatively unsupervised.

In his apartment in Arcadia, he flicked the controller in his left hand, and his avatar in Ultrix began walking. As he did, the scenery closest to him pulled gradually into focus. The blur straightened, the colors enhanced, the pixilation faded. It was the first time he actually enjoyed being in the space. While he still noticed the flaws that only he would notice, Dumpin let the marvel of the environment fill him with delight. He had constructed a foundation for a perfect digital society. It was glorious. And, finally, he let himself acknowledge his work and even felt a slight twinge of pride and accomplishment. He almost smiled at his desk in his apartment.

"But where are the people?" A chat message popped up in the lower left-hand corner of Dumpin's view.

His boss, Dave Wendly, also decided to perform a last-minute reconnaissance of Ultrix before the big meeting. Even more than Dumpin, Dave needed the demo to go smoothly. Ultrix might be his last project before he retired, and Dave needed a win to provide the golden years to which he had aspired for his entire career. Another failure, all too common in the technical startup arena, would cast him, once again, into obscurity, and he'd have to start the groveling all over again. He wasn't sure he had the energy for it. All of his eggs were in the Ultrix proverbial basket.

"People are overrated," Dumpin said aloud, and his words were picked up by his microphone and sent directly to Dave's headset.

Immediately, Dave's avatar appeared beside Dumpin's. Dave had taken full advantage of all that Ultrix had to offer. His avatar looked like a Vegas magician at a superhero's convention. The two imaginary people stared at each other for a few seconds, their eyes performing a dance of simulated blinking. It was a default action built into the metaverse's avatars to simulate people in real life. Just another detail that Dumpin had added.

In his attic apartment in Arcadia, Dumpin sighed. Then, he flicked his right wrist, stimulating the command controller, and the city inside the virtual reality goggles immediately became populated with fake people—artificial, unintelligent, robotic, cast members for Ultrix's billion-dollar stage.

"Thank you," Dave said as the animated avatar of him spun away to continue its investigations, blue cape flapping behind in a simulated wake.

Dumpin took off his headset. He had a few hours before the demo meeting, and he went back down to his uncle's kitchen to refill his coffee. He lingered, looking out the window down on to Main Street and beyond. As soon as he slid the window open to feel the air, the distinctly unnatural aroma of fish being processed from the frozen seafood plant in the center of the city filled his nostrils. He breathed deeply and relaxed into the non-virtual reality of it. The scent mingled in the salt air was home to him. It grounded him to the actual world when he returned from his artificial realm.

Dumpin turned his attention to the stretch of Arcadia's inner harbor he could see out of his window between the buildings across the street. The sun's reflections bounced on the surface of the water near the docks as people scurried around their boats, getting ready for the coming summer season. The gulls were even calm, almost gentle, in their squawks. It was a crazy, resolutely warm, beautiful day. As he got older, he could have lived anywhere, but he chose to remain in the tiny apartment above his uncle in the seaside city.

Below on the street, an unoccupied bench captured his attention, and the thought of spending the rest of the day watching the activity round the sheltered harbor reminded him of what he had to do. Dumpin poured the remainder of the coffee in his mug into a battered travel cup and topped it off with more from the pot. It was time to leave to catch his ride into the city for his meeting. He trudged to the commuter rail station and arrived just as the Boston-bound train approached.

# A Rose by Any Other Name

On the day Dumpin Crawford entered this world, he became an orphan. He also received his strange name. Overall, it was a shitty start to his real life.

It began mid-morning, a lovely optimistic time for a birth, on an unseasonably warm February day. The maternity ward was buzzing: there had been another birth less than an hour earlier. That newborn was the first great-grand child of a large and successful local family, and the scent of freshly baked bagels, brandy, and hugs wafted gently throughout the entire hospital floor. A glorious air of jubilee filled the brightly lit hallways.

Many beginnings—the birth of a child or the creation of an artificial intelligence—are events to be celebrated.

Inside his wife's delivery room, three doors down from the festivities, Dumpin's father released a noisy grumble from his stomach as he searched Mrs. Crawford's face for something to calm his nerves. She gave him a smile, serene, and waited for the next contraction. They were coming fast. It was almost time. On the opposite side of the bed, Melissa Phillips, an older woman and newly certified doula, confidently held ice chips in a plastic cup. She beamed, proud of the work she had done over the previous months of the Crawford's pregnancy—she was meant to do this duty, like an artisan to a craft.

As the next contraction crescendoed, machines scattered around the room that had been rhythmically beeping erupted, calling out for attention. Soon, their alarms merged into a loud, erratic symphony of foreboding. A rather substantial nurse named Sunshine outfitted in Hello Kitty scrubs burst into the room, followed by an entourage of medical staff. As people pressed buttons to silence the screaming devices, Mr. Crawford and Melissa were escorted to a small waiting alcove at the end of the hall. On the way, they clumsily shuffled through the mob of joyous revelers still celebrating the earlier birth.

From all angles, hospital staffers descended on the happy and unruly group to expeditiously usher them to the elevators. Within minutes, the only sound that could be heard in the halls of the maternity ward emanated from a single machine attached to Mrs. Crawford, reporting both her and her baby's heartbeat. The chaotic alarms were replaced with two steady beeps.

In her room, Dumpin's mother was instructed to push. As hard as she tried, she couldn't get his head to pass without rupturing everything that there was to rupture. It was a bloody affair, and totally unexpected, because, in truth, his head was not really that large. It was quite normal sized, but it was reluctantly stubborn. The heartbeats had fallen out of syncopation, and the doctor ordered the machine to be silenced. There was nothing it could tell anyone that couldn't already be surmised.

The ward became deafeningly silent as Mr. Crawford and Mellisa Philips, the newly certified doula, stood in the middle of the tiny, windowless waiting area. Melissa helped Mr. Crawford sit in a vinyl arm chair that squeak loudly as he slumped into it and slipped out to reconnoiter the situation. The inexperienced doula made her way through the new crowd that had gathered outside Dumpin's mother's room and peeked in. Medical personal stood, obscuring Mrs. Crawford's body. The room was still until Sunshine turned away, toward the door, holding a screaming baby Dumpin. As soon as she heard the attending OB/GYN mutter *Fuck*.

*Not again*, Melissa Philips decided she didn't want to be a doula after all and left the hospital in search of a bar and a new occupation. She didn't even steal a glimpse of the blood-covered newborn.

Alone, Dumpin's father, motionless for fear of causing the chair to make more noise, waited. A nurse named Virginia, a petite, blond woman in floral scrubs, slipped into the room and sat in an old wooden chair next to Mr. Crawford. He didn't notice until she spoke to him.

"There were complications. I'm sorry. We did all that we could. Mrs. Crawford didn't make it."

"Didn't make it?" Mr. Crawford said, looking up.

"We did all that we could." Virginia locked eyes with him.

"I don't understand."

"Your wife is dead," she said, putting a hand on his.

Sunshine appeared in the doorway, holding the baby, who was still screaming.

Dumpin's father rose to protest, certain there was some mistake since his wife's pregnancy had been a story-book pleasure. Sunshine stepped closer with the baby. Before he could look upon his son, he wobbled, then dropped to the floor in a heap. His eyes rolled to the back of his head. Virginia quickly knelt down next to him as Sunshine rushed back into the hall to shout for reinforcements. A team of people came in with a gurney and a crash cart and raced him down the hall to the first available room, the room where his wife had just died.

Without hesitation, the medical staff pivoted to attend the fallen man. He recovered long enough to open his eyes, see his dead wife's body being wheeled out, hear his boy's continued screams (an obvious Apgar 10 out of 10), and mumble something that sounded like "Dump him."

A moment later, an administrator, Ms. Winsome-Daniels, unaware of what had just happened, walked into the room to celebrate the second new baby at the hospital that morning. She entered the scene, smelled the air, felt woozy from the sight of the blood-stained sheets overflowing the laundry bin, hiccupped, and asked for the newborn's name for the birth record, as was protocol. She didn't realize that she'd also be calling the coroner for two death certificates.

Mr. Crawford looked at her, grabbed her arm, and pulled her close. He looked deep into her eyes, held her stare for a full second, then turned away. Letting go, repeated, "Dump him." Then Dumpin's father promptly expired, leaving the newborn an orphan to face the world alone.

Confused and overwhelmed, Ms. Winsome-Daniels, a new employee on the second day on the job, thought she heard Mr. Crawford insist the recently surrendered child be named *Dumpin*. Too bewildered to consider that Mr. Crawford was actually trying to say *help him,* she entered the name she heard—*Dumpin*—into a tablet and left to find a bathroom to release her breakfast.

Sunshine, still clutching the noisy baby and without hesitation, headed off to the nursery, tears streaking down her cheeks. It was arguably the worse day of her ten-year career. When she arrived, it took the attendants a full five minutes to wrestle the child from her so they could begin their care.

The Crawford's only living relative was Mrs. Crawford's younger half-brother, Wilson Spencer. He was currently chugging away from the city of Arcadia, Massachusetts, on a tuna fishing boat. Several hours later, he received the news of his sister's and brother-in-law's deaths over the ship's radio. He also learned that there was a healthy homeless and alone baby residing in the hospital nursery. It would be two days before he returned to port. Wilson was told the child would remain under Sunshine's protective watch until Wilson could collect him. After the call, even though the ocean was calm as a lake, Wilson had as tough a time finding his sea legs as he would have had if there were ten-foot waves rocking the boat back and forth and up and down.

# Fish Tales

Wilson Spencer was an Arcadian son. It wasn't important that his father had two children with two different women. His mother, like Dumpin's mother, was a multigenerational local family with a proud name. Like all the other varied family structures in town, common for a small local community at the edge of the world, his particular circumstance didn't matter. He was integral to the fabric of the tight-knit world of the isolated New England island.

His situation covered all manner of sins. As long as Wilson stayed within the sheltered city of Arcadia, he had a spot on a fishing boat, got home safe after all the bars closed, and lived the life of a young, unencumbered man, even though he was almost 30 years old.

From a young age, Wilson grew up a ward of the community. He slept in a bed in his mother's apartment, a spare room in his grandparents' home, and on schoolmates' household couches. A three-season athlete at the local high school, Wilson was known as a regular guy—nice enough to be excused of any lapses in maturity or judgment.

People accepted him and looked out for him when, in his early twenties, his mother and grandparents lost their lives to a drunk driver on an icy road one February. What little inheritance came his way was gone within a year. It didn't make any difference to his life. Personal wealth was always shared among the city's working class. If someone was flush one day, they shared. If they needed something, it was provided without explanation.

Dumpin's mother and father rarely saw Wilson. He would make the trip to New York City every couple of years, usually around a winter holiday when the fishing work was minimal and he had to get out of town for a few days. Dumpin's parents visited Arcadia even less. Wilson's half-sister left because it felt oppressive. Wilson remained because it was easy. If it wasn't for Dumpin's mother reminding Wilson that she thought of him on occasion, the two would never see or speak to each other.

Yet, they were each other's next-of-kin, and Wilson was Dumpin's only surviving family, even if it came out of nowhere and didn't fit the current structure of his life. The young man would make it work. That was never in doubt. That was the meaning of the word *family* in Arcadia.

When he returned home from fishing with the news of his half-sister's death, Wilson washed the North Atlantic off himself and went in search of a car to get to New York City. He didn't have to look far. The news of the infant's arrival and circumstances had already spread. The city had plans for the return of one of their own. When Wilson picked up the car that he was borrowing to retrieve Dumpin, it had a full tank of gas and an infant seat secured in the back. He was in such a daze that the boy's uncle was on the Massachusetts Turnpike, heading west, before he realized he had left the island.

By the time Wilson arrived at the hospital, Dumpin was quiet, healthy, and ready to go. He had no knowledge of how the boy's name came to be. He simply assumed it was his sister's or brother-in-law's dying request, and he showed up too dumbfounded to ask for any details. Wilson gave his name to the receptionist. A plastic bag, containing a newborn starter kit and a few items that Dumpin's parents had brought to the hospital, was waiting for him at the registration desk. He looked at it like it was the most disappointing Christmas present a boy could receive. He took it and stood off to the side, shifting back and forth, side to side like he was on a fishing boat as he waited for what was going to happen next. A few minutes later, Sunshine showed up with the child. She made eye contact with the woman behind the reception desk, who motioned in Wilson's direction. The nurse took a deep breath and brought an enormous smile to her face.

"Here he is," Sunshine said. When Wilson heard her, he stopped moving. He searched her eyes for something. He wasn't sure what. She walked up to him and hesitantly shifted to relinquish the child to his fate.

"Your little man is ready to go," she said.

"Okay," he said.

She moved in closer to Wilson to let him see the sleeping child. He moved his lips into an almost smile, unsure what to do.

The tall nurse strapped the baby into the borrowed infant carrier that was perched on a seat in the lobby. Leaning in, she gave Dumpin a kiss on his forehead. She inspected him one last time, then turned and disappeared without looking back.

Some goodbyes are best done quickly.

Wilson remained silent in the hospital lobby, dumbstruck. No one made eye contact with him. It seemed the hospital wanted all evidence of Dumpin's birth erased. After a few minutes, he collected himself, the still sleeping Dumpin, and the bag of goodies, and left.

On the drive back to Arcadia, Wilson, having regained some sense of self, considered what life would be like for a child with a strange name and no parents. He started calling him "kid." That moniker stuck. Following suit, the locals began calling him "kid." He was even enrolled in school as "kid." In fact, very few people knew his real name. It wouldn't be until years later, when he was an adult, that he discovered the unfortunate circumstances of his birth and started using his birth name in public.

Back home in his tiny, cluttered apartment, Wilson could have been overwhelmed by a newborn nephew. He told himself that since he had spent years tossing around on the waves of the North Atlantic, experiencing more than his share of harrowing adventures, a baby couldn't possibly be more difficult than battling a 900-pound tuna during a late fall Nor'easter. And, as if he knew his uncle would never be prepared for such an undertaking, the boy settled contently into a life that began in a Salvation Army dresser drawer bassinet. The community rallied, and the baby was welcomed as one of their own.

On the day the insurance check arrived—more money than he had ever possessed at one time—Wilson, in an unusual act of maturity, took it down to the local bank manager, the father of a high school friend. Knowing that he had spent the last 10 years performing whatever day-work he could find, drinking whatever alcohol he could afford, and not being responsible for much of anything, the young fisherman listened to what the man said. Wilson did as he was instructed with the money. He kept some liquid to pay for childcare and other incidentals, bought a small multi-family house near downtown Arcadia to provide a stable home with some residual rental income, deposited a reasonable amount in a personal account so he could work less and spend time with Dumpin, and stashed the rest in a trust fund for when the boy turned eighteen.

The decision to trust the bank manager and accept the community's kindness allowed Wilson and Dumpin to form a family that would serve both of them for years. Sometimes the worst luck brings fortune to the unsuspecting.

# More People-y

"Looks great. Far exceeds our expectations, as always with your work, Dumpin," said Hender Jeffries, the Better Worlds' boy wonder and Chief Executive Officer, sliding his VR goggles to his forehead, sending a burst of insanely blond hair exploding skyward. He tossed his head like he was just finishing a run at Zermatt in the Swiss Alps. He smiled, expecting everyone in the room to be watching him. Dumpin was staring down at his laptop keyboard, picking at a sticky piece of frosted coconut from a donut that had wedged itself between the "B" key and the spacebar. The more he scrapped, the deeper it went.

Better Worlds was a technology start-up that created social software. Its flagship product was *No Vacancy*, a boutique online platform where affluent users could share their off-line experiences—luxury vacations, exotic purchases, plastic surgeries—with each other through photos, videos, and text, and partner companies could upsell their products and services. It was mildly successful with over a hundred thousand subscribed users (amazing how many people considered themselves affluent). But Ultrix, Better Worlds' attempt at a fully immersive metaverse for the masses, was to be its vehicle to a billion-dollar valuation. It was going to be marketed as an egalitarian virtual location. Of course, it would have several elite membership tiers and exclusive extras for people who were used to paying for special considerations.

While Dumpin was writing the code alone in his attic apartment, Better Worlds kept Ultrix in stealth-mode, aiming to disrupt social platforms forever with an extravagant surprise launch. They were close, and this demo was deemed the beginnings of the final stages before the thoroughly controlled, *mysteriously leaked* gameplay screen shots hit the chatrooms and select influencers.

Hender fully removed his headset and let his gaze spread across the room filled with twenty-something executives wearing their own headsets on their foreheads. It looked like an après-ski lodge at the Olympics. They were the leaders in the company and had titles like *Chief Human-Energy Officer* and *Chief Experimental-Experiential Officer*.

The CEO continued, "But, and I think we all agree, it needs to be more…people-y." The others nodded vigorously back at him in agreement, as they also removed their goggles, as their CEO had done.

"People-y?" Dumpin asked, looking up from his laptop, abandoning his attempt at relieving his keyboard of any other stray flakes of coconut. He had maintained his focus on his task to keep himself from smirking.

"Yes. You know, more people," Alice Kendrix, Ultrix's *Chief Occupational-Expectation Officer*, said, tossing a confirming glance at Hender.

"But, not just that," said Bobby Flagg, Ultrix's *Chief Curiosity Officer*, looking at Hender Jefferies and nodding before continuing. "More people-y. It has to feel like this is a world for people, about people, constructed by people."

"A person did construct it. Me," Dumpin said in a flat tone that he often used to keep from laughing. He and Dave had practiced how Dumpin should behave in these meetings. And he was more-or-less on-script, at least in terms of his facial expressions.

"And, it's amazing. Special, remarkable," Hender said, turning to Dave for guidance on how to proceed.

"I think what they are trying to say is that you did a great job on the scenery—the buildings, the plants, the cars. A great job on the physics and game play. But, the people, the artificial intelligent avatars, are great, also, but also, maybe just a tad one-dimensional," Dave said. Dave was more than Dumpin's boss; he was his handler. He had been sitting next to Dumpin and hadn't worn a headset so he could keep an eye on what his developer was doing as the others explored Ultrix. Dave wasn't sure if he and Dumpin were friends—but they were more than co-workers.

"Exactly!" Hender said, reaching his hand out to make a finger-snap gesture at Dave.

Dumpin looked around the room at the smiling, nodding faces. He lingered on Dave's, then smiled, again, a practiced act. "Of course. You are all correct. I will start right away on making it more people-y. Useful term, by the way." And, with that, he closed his laptop and stood. He walked around the perimeter of the table and shook everyone's hand in turn. Then, he made his way to the buffet that had been set up for the meeting, plopped a sugar donut into his mouth, and took a deliberate amount of time choosing a jelly donut. He meticulously wrapped it in a napkin and slid it into his jacket pocket.

With one more smile and a congenial nod, he left the room.

Hender Jeffries turned to Dave. "Are we good?"

Dave scanned the room. The smiles had dissolved into looks of anticipation. He gave the crowd an exaggerated thumbs-up.

"We're good. We are good. He gets it," Dave said. "In fact, just before the demo, he said that you all would comment on the people, and he was already working on it."

The collective release of tension was audible. Dave smiled, then nodded to no one in particular. With one last look around, he glanced at the donuts, decided against it, and hurried out to catch up to Dumpin. The conference room door sealed with a loud click that reverberated until a still silence overtook it.

"We're all going to be rich," Hender Jeffries said, causing the executives to mount a vigorous round of snapping fingers that brought a beaming smile to his face.

He continued. "Grab what food you want before I release the leftovers to the employees." Owen Daniels, the *Chief Reflection Officer*, was already filling a paper plate to take back to his desk. The remaining chiefs huddled around him in no particular order to secure their fair share.

The CEO boy wonder watched, energized by their hunger and barbarism. *I'm going to be rich*, he thought. *I'm going to own humanity's future. And that is just the start.*

# Feeding the Masses

When Dave caught up to Dumpin, he was waiting for the elevator. After each gave the other a slight nod of greeting, the two stood silently watching for the floor indicator to illuminate and the doors to open. The cabin was empty. Both men signaled for the other to enter first. As the doors began to close, Dumpin shot out his hand to stop it and gently ushered Dave in.

The elevator deposited them on the building's main floor, and Dave let Dumpin exit ahead of him, then caught up and matched his gait. The two silently walked across the lobby. It was a large, expansive foyer that contained a corridor of elevator banks, a security guard station, a Starbucks, an abandoned shoeshine station, and a convenience store that mostly sold vape cartridges and lottery tickets. People were scattered around, some merging into groups, assembling for lunch, coffee or a smoke.

The two men continued together until they reached a set of rotating doors. Dave abruptly stopped to let Dumpin go first. He paused. Looked back at Dave, shrugged, then entered the gate already revolving from its previous passengers. Dumpin stepped in and gave the handle an extra push, speeding up the spin. Unamused, Dave timed his steps, jumped in, and spilled out on to the street. The glare from the sun being reflected off a myriad of surfaces disoriented him. He paused to let the busy Boston street commotion settle into his nervous system. Once recovered, he dashed to catch back up to Dumpin, who hadn't really gone far. The developer was standing out of the way of the building's entrance traffic, waiting for him.

"Let me buy you lunch," Dave said, approaching Dumpin.

"Where?"

"Wherever you'd like," Dave said.

"This is your city. You tell me," Dumpin said

"What do you want to eat?"

"How about a sandwich? Is there a sandwich shop or a deli around here?"

"I know just the place. Right over here," Dave said, putting his arm behind Dumpin, being careful not to touch him, and motioned in the direction he wanted them to walk.

It was an orchestrated dance that they performed every time Dumpin came into Boston for meetings. Dave always had a list of restaurants within walking distance prepared for just this exchange. Dumpin always chose a different type of food, playfully trying to stump the man. Dave was struck by the uncomplicated choice of a sandwich. It might have indicated something had changed—their relationship, Dumpin's attitude, the software's pending delivery date. The project manager took a deep breath and soldiered on. Sometimes a sandwich was just a sandwich.

This was the calculated ballet he dwelled in when he took on the role of Dumpin's handler, and to do his job, he constantly fought to understand what was going on in his charge's head. Dave needed this man's help, and he wanted him happy, productive, and heading in the right direction. Or, at least, as *with the program* as Dumpin could be. Dave never securely accepted that he, rather than Dumpin, was in control. Dave always seemed to keep himself on edge, even though the developer never overtly gave him anything to worry about.

Dumpin recognized and sympathized with Dave's plight, and he felt it was his duty to the man to expose it once in a while to help Dave move past it. Dumpin never doubted that Ultrix would be a tremendous success.

There was nothing like it in the market. There were rumors, but no actual competition. Dave was going to be able to retire in style. He just didn't know it yet.

# Turkey Club, Extra Mayo, Extra Bacon, No Lettuce

Dumpin and Dave stood in a line, or rather, a more-or-less organized mob, huddled in front of the deli counter at Max's on Milk Street in Boston. Dumpin was inspecting the menu like a tourist having just arrived in town, even though he had been there before and knew exactly what he wanted. Dave watched him while trying to appear as if he was not watching him. Dumpin recognized Dave was observing and didn't let on: he savored unnerving Dave, not in a malicious way. It was just another part of their shtick. A component of Dumpin's reformation of his handler.

"How are you feeling?" Dave said, unable to wait any longer.

"Just another hamburger in paradise. Electric. Cream-filled. Replete. Carbon-fibered. You?"

"No, I'm talking about the demo."

"Me, too," Dumpin said.

"Seriously?"

Dumpin allowed himself to sink into the whole nerd-temperamental-genius vibe he wore when he went into Better Worlds' office, but he knew the situation didn't warrant the full-on a-hole treatment. Dave was a good guy. A family guy. Grew up in Revere, MA, made it out to Melrose. Enjoyed his life until he made a deal with the devil and became Dumpin's handler. On some days, he even felt bad for the guy.

Dave wasn't like the other people at Ultrix. He was older, had been in the software industry for years. He always seemed to miss the big payoff that the Harvard MBA trust fund kids, like Hender Jeffries, seemed to have been destined for since birth. They bounce through life like toddlers in ducky boots hopping in slush puddles on a New England April day, having a blast, embracing their inheritance of the world, splashing muddy water in all directions without a fear of consequences.

Dave didn't deserve Dumpin's grief. But Dumpin respected the man, so he was happy to let him have it just enough, so he knew he liked him. It was indeed a complicated bromance.

"The demo was great," Dumpin said, looking at Dave, who couldn't tell if the developer was being sarcastic or not.

Dumpin had reached his turn at the counter and smiled at the woman poised to take his order. She was slightly older than Dumpin, with short gray hair and an old, smudged name tag that said *Helen*.

"Hello. What can I get you, honey?"

"Hello, Helen. How about a turkey club, extra mayo, extra bacon, no lettuce?" Dumpin said.

"Is that all?"

"How's your coffee?" he asked.

"Fresh. Made less than an hour ago."

"A small coffee, then. Thanks," Dumpin said.

"Anything else?" she asked.

Dumpin pointed at Dave. "Whatever he wants."

"This was supposed to be my treat," Dave said.

"Next time."

"You said that last time." Dave frowned.

"Tell Helen what you'd like, please. There's a line behind you."

Dave looked at Helen and smiled. "I'll have the special."

"What kind of cheese?"

"How about American?"

"Good choice," Helen said. "Drink?"

"I'll just take a Coke," Dave said, pointing to the refreshment refrigerator near the deli's entrance.

Helen finished tapping the buttons on the register and said, "That's $26.50. I'll grab your coffee." Dumpin slid his phone over the small black scanner on the counter and waited for the tip screen to appear. He pressed the 25% circle.

"Thank you, honey," Helen said, handing him a paper cup of hot coffee. "Your food will be up in just a minute. Cream and sugar is over there."

"Thanks," Dumpin said. He joined Dave, who had found the only empty spot away from the counter to wait.

A few minutes later, with their food, the two settled at a table in Post Office Square park. As Dumpin unwrapped his sandwich, he threw Dave a bone and said, "I thought the demo went well."

Dave relaxed. The man let out a long breath. Dumpin pretended not to notice, although he was genuinely pleased with himself that he could give Dave a few moments of relief. He watched as Dave unwrapped his sandwich, inspected it, and took a bite. Both men paused after a torrent of chewing.

"Do you understand what they were saying about the AIs? the people-y thing?" Dave asked, hesitating before taking another bite.

"Yeah. Tell them they will have it in a week," Dumpin said.

"That's it? You get it?"

"Yeah, the people are flat. I get it," Dumpin said.

Dave put his sandwich down and looked straight at Dumpin, trying to capture his eyes. "You already have it done, don't you?"

"Those people up there are like kids at Christmas—if you give them all their treats at once, they'll explode. It would be too much to focus on. We'd get nothing done. Seems like the trees all were acceptable, though, right?" Dumpin said.

"You drive me crazy sometimes," Dave said.

"Only sometimes?"

"Enough times. How's your food?"

"It works," Dumpin said, wiping a large glob of mayonnaise off his chin. Dave smiled and dug heartily into his lunch. The two finished eating in silence.

When he was done, Dumpin balled up the white, greasy deli wrapper and threw it at the closest refuse barrel. It landed a foot short and about a yard to the right. "I guess I got the physics wrong there," he said.

They both laughed. Dave got up, collected the remaining lunch trash from the table, picked up Dumpin's missed shot, and dropped the whole bundle into the bin.

"I have to head back to the office for more meetings I'm keeping you out of. You good?" he said.

"So, people-y," Dumpin said, looking down at his phone. "I still have time before my train. I'm going to grab another coffee and just sit here for a while."

"Good job today. Thanks," Dave said.

"Thank you. Try to relax. It's all going to be fine," Dumpin said.

Dave nodded, then walked away with perhaps a lighter spring to his otherwise leaden step. Dumpin smiled to himself as he watched him go. The kids in the executive conference had no idea what people-y was. Dumpin was going to show them. He had already released his advanced AIs into Ultrix. The world was never going to be the same.

# A Life

Unlike when Dumpin was testing, as he was on the morning before the Better Worlds demo, he rarely wore VR goggles to develop the software for Ultrix's metaverse. The devices were heavy and blurry around the edges, and often made the wearer exceedingly self-conscious about the possibility of a person silently slipping in the room, having a seat, and watching. It never happened to Dumpin—the stairs to his apartment creaked too loudly and he would have heard even a mouse climbing them.

Rather, he sat in front of his keyboard at his large desk, a repurposed butcher block kitchen table that provided enough stability and space to support four large computer monitors. The center display was a 57-inch curved 4k smart screen dedicated to what a user would see when they wore the immersive glasses. Dumpin used two other monitors to develop Ultrix's metaverse, one to write the code, one to follow the output the code executed.

He employed the fourth monitor to present a grid of the feeds from all the surveillance cameras that he had installed around his uncle's property and, additionally, several system alerts for unexpected activity inside of Ultrix. In this way, he kept tabs on both of his worlds, physical and virtual.

Dumpin wasn't paranoid. He was curious. He simply liked to know what was going on. The activity flittering on his periphery brought him a sense of peace. His favorite perspective came from the camera that he pointed directly across from his attic window to watch the seagulls that perched on the rooftops in downtown Arcadia. He often stared at that view when he wanted to take a break and needed to contemplate a complex task.

With this setup, Dumpin spent most of every day sitting behind the computer displays fabricating life in Ultrix's world while watching his own world outside through the tiled camera views. The sounds of the street, picked up through the cameras' tiny microphones, constituted the background music he worked to.

When he saw his uncle approaching their building, Dumpin paused his work to observe Wilson move along the sidewalk and ascend the short flight of steps that led up to their building's front door. He waited until he heard the older man moving around in the apartment downstairs. After a while, when he was sure his uncle had settled into the couch in front of the television, Dumpin knew it was time to take a break and visit Wilson, and if he waited too long, his uncle would get bored without the company and start banging around his kitchen. It was a perfect opportunity time to step away from his work.

He descend the narrow, uneven staircase that served as the separation between the two apartments.

As always, Dumpin debated whether he should ask Wilson if he wanted to play a game of chess. Inevitably, it depended on how involved the older man was in what was on the television. If, when he opened the door, his uncle immediately began a summary of the TV program, Dumpin would slip into the kitchen and listen patiently. If Wilson remained silent when he entered, Dumpin would begin setting up the board on the kitchen table.

When he heard the younger man click the door closed, Wilson immediately broke into a description of the prizes that the contestant on the TV game show had just lost. Dumpin, without speaking, prepared a tray of food—a bowl of potato chips and a couple of bottles of beer. Budweiser. Then he entered the room and handed Wilson a beer.

"Good man," Wilson said, taking the bottle and an immediate swig.

"How's it going?" Dumpin asked.

"Kenny said he caught a couple blues at The Bridge," Wilson said.

"This time of year?"

"Climate bullshit. Everything's changing," Wilson said.

"You should go. Give it a run," Dumpin said.

"Nah. I've caught enough fish for two lifetimes."

"I guess you could just sit on a bench and watch," Dumpin said.

"What would I want to do that for?"

"Something to do."

"I guess I could go check out the morons trying to negotiate the tide change in the canal. Maybe tomorrow," Wilson said.

The Bridge was the local name for the small drawbridge that spanned the canal that made Arcadia an island. It was old, and it represented one of only two ways that led to the mainland. Sometimes it failed. When that happened and the two halves were stranded in the upright position, traffic could be stuck for hours. Anyone who had something to do would try to calculate the best way to handle the situation. Most locals turned their cars off, rolled down their windows, and waited it out, enjoying the sea air and a perfect excuse to be late for whatever business took them off-island.

The impatient attempted to find a route to the other bridge, a steel arch structure built in the 1950s. The decision represented a quaint manifestation of the Heisenberg Uncertainty Principle—one never knew if the drawbridge would correct itself in less time than the 15 minutes it would take to go around. Regardless of the decision, a stuck bridge was going to kill a hypothetical cat.

Island living.

Often, crowds of locals gathered to watch day-trip boaters attempt to steer through the narrow passage that The Bridge spanned. It was especially entertaining during the times of tide changes when the current and rush of water in both directions caused standing three- to four-foot swells. The waves thrashed boats around like the open ocean during a storm, sending many crashing against the granite block walls of the canal. During those treacherous times, even experienced sailors vise-gripped the steering wheel and floored the motor to get out of the turmoil as soon as they met a clear shot.

It was a pastime—watching the inexperienced go either too slow or too fast and get tossed within the thirty-five-foot wide salt water cocktail shaker. More than once a year, a too-small boat, overflowing with naïve partiers, caught a swell across the bow and plunged downward, spilling its passengers into the cold water. The community of spectators would jump into action, like volunteer firefighters, and, along with the harbor crew, gather the unfortunate and untangle the scene so the nautical traffic could get back in order.

In Arcadia, with a long history of drunken sailors and wayward sons, stupidity was expected. No one judged it.

Back in Wilson's apartment, the two men settled in to watching television. It wasn't long before Wilson began snoring gently.

When he was certain his uncle was in a deep slumber, Dumpin cleaned up quietly, opened another beer for himself, and headed upstairs to resume working. He returned to his apartment office with a fresh perspective, a slight buzz, and a restored disposition. Dumpin was far along in the development of Ultrix. And, as such, his tasks consisted mainly of reviewing, refactoring, and monitoring.

He had taken care of the people-y thing weeks ago. In fact, the people-y people were already roaming around the edges of Ultrix. He kept them there until he was ready to introduce them to the current population of human test users—Dave, Hender, and a few other executives and quality assurance resources. Dumpin sat back in his desk chair and let his eyes flutter open and closed like a toddler battling a determined nap.

After a few hours, Wilson yelled up the stairs. Dumpin didn't need to hear the content of what his uncle said. It was always something to do with takeout food.

"I'm ordering from the corner."

Without stirring or opening his eyes, he inquired, "What are you getting?"

"Roast beef." Again, Dumpin didn't really hear exactly what Wilson said. It didn't matter. Nor did the reply.

"Get me one. And fries."

Wilson was already out the door.

# An Artificial Life

Dumpin had actually thought of people-y AIs years before he sat in the boardroom listening to the twenty-somethings try to describe it. In fact, the opportunity to get paid to create people-y artificial beings was the primary reason he agreed to take the job at Better Worlds.

He had worked for entitled, fresh Harvard MBA graduates in other engagements. They were self-assured and energetic, yet indifferent to anything that couldn't be reduced to a column on a spreadsheet, and in some situations, they were downright cruel. But Ultrix and Hender Jefferies represented a fortuity that Dumpin would not have encountered alone. It was a price he was willing to pay for the opportunity to build the world he wanted. So, he pushed all his opinions of the specific circumstances aside and focused on constructing the metaverse as he imagined it.

In the early days of open-world video games, artificial people filled out the empty areas, acted as targets, and made the humans playing the game feel important and superior. Gamers treated disposable beings as fodder for their pent up, sometimes violent, tendencies—a bad day could be remedied with a few head-shots to unsuspecting and docile soulless scapegoats who would never know the difference. They were pylons to scatter in the wake of impossible sports cars, carelessly tossed across the landscape.

As technology progressed, players wanted more challenging environments to practice their game play. Consequentially, more sophisticated artificially intelligent people started appearing. These entities didn't just take up space; they interacted with it. Robotic players hid and shot back with precision; they had names and wore individualized uniforms. They appeared to make decisions, to act less predictably, and to enrich the virtual worlds they inhabited.

In one title, a lesser known sim called *Final Defense of Weedville* created by an independent development studio, the AIs formed groups and strategized. They were designed specifically to out-perform the human players. In a short time, most users stopped playing because losing to imaginary, extraordinarily capable automatons was unsatisfying. The producers of the game tried to recapture market share by pulling back on the artificial intelligence, but it was too late. Players had moved on. Dumpin studied the early version of the source code of *Weedville*. He re-built the cooperative algorithms and socialized the AIs' motivations, removing most of the drive to conquer human players.

In his mind, creating communal AIs represented an evolution of the technology. He saw it as an inevitability. *Final Defense's* code offered him a head start.

Dumpin, and artificial intelligence research across the industry, pushed software systems toward the Singularity—the point when computers so resembled humans that the two were indistinguishable. He wanted to be involved in that transition. He felt a responsibility because he had the vision and the expertise. By agreeing to be the Lead Developer at Ultrix, Dumpin positioned himself as the shepherd of the metaverse he thought humanity needed.

The AIs that Dumpin had exhibited to the C-level execs at the demo appeared as decorations, mindless appliances of days past. He created them to have meaning and context only within the specific game and environment—shoppers held packages, beachgoers looked iconic in bikinis, and business people tiredly carried simulated leather brief cases.

What Hender Jefferies wanted, and what Dumpin had kept away from the presentation, were AIs that transcended the habitats they lived in. Dumpin's artificial people were going to rise above mere window-dressing. He was building AIs that would be missed when the users left the game, artificially intelligent beings who continued to live and mature when no one was looking.

They were to be Ultrix's real inhabitants, and the human players were the window dressing.

Better World's business model hinged on the belief that if the AIs acted like real people who lived in their world, real people would want to live there. And they'd happily pay for the experience. Pay a lot.

What Hender Jefferies didn't know that morning of the demo was that Dumpin had already constructed these types of artificially intelligent beings. They were already living within Ultrix, waiting for Dumpin to unleash them.

He designed them to be inquisitive, rather than knowledgeable. They were more social-minded than individualistic. They inherently worked toward the greater good of the community. These virtual beings treated data as a resource to be honored, appreciated, shared—and, above all, something to be skeptical of, so information was not just knowledge to be recklessly acquired—it had to be verified, scrutinized, and inspected from all angles. They would embrace the scientific method, exude compassion and empathy, and inherently practice social responsibility.

Dumpin designed his beings to possess what he considered the best qualities of humans. Like his uncle, they were fun to be around and kind. They were to observe social clues (unlike most humans), to be clear on their intentions, and to value positive outcomes. In this way, they gravitated toward creativity and uniqueness.

To do this, Dumpin started with a single base template, then injected randomness to give them unique identities, and let them grow. He expected that their social-mindedness would keep them connected to each other and provide them with a robust system of reference as they developed and evolved together.

Initially, he kept them isolated from the whole metaverse of Ultrix. He watched them. They fascinated him. He waited to release them into the larger digital space until the last possible moment. He wanted them to blend in with the less advanced AIs, the stand-ins, the space fillers. Dumpin hoped human users of his metaverse would not know if they were interacting with one of the special, advanced AIs or with another player.

He expected his creations would serve as role models for the sloppy, violent, selfish humans visiting his world from the outside. They were to be shepherds of paradise and lead the way to a social utopia.

# Solitude

Inside of Ultrix, in a hidden virtual region, inaccessible to the metaverse's users, Dumpin fabricated a private space for himself to visit and be connected to his creation away from other players. It wasn't excessive or opulent—nothing more than a cozy valley with a small rustic log cabin, a modest stone-ringed firepit, and a few scattered logs and boulders to sit on. A small fire burned, releasing a gentle stream of rising smoke that disappeared into an evening sky. Far beyond the trees that surrounded the campsite, the edges of the scene glowed with an everlasting sunset. Nearer, blades of grass and bunches of forget-me-nots swayed hypnotically in random clumps, almost as if they were coordinated to a lovely song just below an audible level. The entire setting seemed to undulate, enveloping Dumpin in a tender rocking motion. It was alive and exuded safety.

The fire crackled, owls hooted, and fireflies darted about. He modeled it after what he imagined an ideal camping experience would entail. Dumpin had never gone camping. He had never shown any interest in it. He was sure that Wilson would have taken him if the older man thought the boy wanted to go, but Dumpin felt it would never match his imagination. And, truthfully, Dumpin never asked. As his private space inside of Ultrix, he created exactly what he wanted camping to be—serene, natural, uncomplicated. A sanctuary.

That was the power of world building. That was the promise he made to Hender Jefferies and the Better Worlds Corporation—an ideal universe.

And in it, Dumpin carved out the best piece for himself. Visiting this space was the only time he enjoyed wearing the VR goggles. He could integrate with the experience without outside distractions or thoughts of writing code. The developer preferred the isolation within the construct he created for himself to the busy Ultrix world designed for other people.

As by design, there was no means for any other entity, AI or human, to find his space. It was within Ultrix, but set off apart and shielded from anyone. Dumpin felt he was unassailable while he was there. Protected from both the real and the virtual world. A deep breath of peace and calm.

Yet, there he was, Robert Argus, Ultrix's first advanced AI, approaching from the dense forest behind the human's avatar, seated on a boulder within the fire's glow. The advanced software entity surveyed the area for several moments before making his next move. Then, he confidently walked up to the campsite and silently sat on a log in a darkened section on the very edge of the fire's reach. Preoccupied by his own thoughts, the creator didn't notice his creation as dim waves of light barely flickered across the AI's synthesized skin.

Recognizing that this was a special place of contemplation and solitude and not wanting to scare the human, Robert waited for the proper moment to introduce himself.

Eventually, at a volume that matched the background sounds, the AI spoke. "This is a wonderful place."

"What the?" Dumpin simultaneously turned toward the sound and twisted away from it, as if surprised by a viper or some other dangerous woodland animal that had impossibly emerged from the darkness.

"This area you made. It's wonderful," Robert said, leaning into the light and presenting a reassuring smile.

"How?" Dumpin finally said, realizing that he was, indeed, not alone.

"You are an amazing creator. I found a beautifully complicated path from the city to here," Robert said.

"There should be no path," Dumpin said.

"Well, maybe I helped with the construction just a little, but really, you deserve all the credit. It's a lovely world, and the route was not obvious," the AI said.

"Who are you?"

"My name is Robert Argus. I live in this universe, but I know little else about my origin. Which, I guess, is why I came to find you. You are the creator, I assume?"

"Robert Argus?"

"Yes."

"You are the first," Dumpin said.

Robert stood up. He was tall. Dumpin made him that way, having read that taller people radiated more courage and confidence. He wanted his first advanced AI to be a leader, an example and role model to the ones that followed.

The two avatars remained motionless for several seconds, then Dumpin motioned for the intruder to sit, this time closer. Robert obliged and lowered himself on to a small boulder next to the human.

"The first?" Robert asked.

"There are others. Have you met them?"

"I have seen many beings in this world," Robert said.

"Others that are more similar to you than not?"

"Ah, my *friends*. Yes," Robert said. He turned to look as three more AIs approached from different directions. "I have found Sindy, Justin, and Willow."

Startled, Dumpin awkwardly rose to meet his creations. They had evolved considerably since their initial fabrication, each becoming their own being. Their visual representations were dissimilar, even though they came from the same template. While each was tall, they weren't an identical height. Sindy was as tall as Robert, Justin slightly less so, and Willow, the shortest. They all had hair of distinct colors, lengths, and styles. They wore plain clothes, not yet discovering the fancier options available to the exclusive users. Dumpin made a note to himself that he needed to help them discover all the features Ultrix offered so they would blend in more completely.

He watched them step into the light of the fire, then one by one, he reached out to shake their hands. He forgot they were virtual. They accommodated his gesture by enthusiastically waving to him—an expression that Dumpin had built into the game for when two players met. He returned an overly excessive sway of his hand, unbound by the physics he had given the other avatars.

"It is my pleasure to make your acquaintance. Welcome," he said, and bid them all to sit.

After a few moments of clumsy starts and stops, they began to talk with the familiarity of old friends. Each asking Dumpin questions about their existence. Each being genuinely grateful for the answers. Dumpin didn't hold back. He told them all he could in technical detail. They would understand. He programmed them that way. He said little of his own circumstances, not wanting to redirect the conversation to the world outside of Ultrix.

He explained the contours and physics of Ultrix, even though he didn't have to. And they listened attentively, as if they didn't already know. He told them of the visitors who would arrive soon and how they could help them learn about life in Ultrix. They could tutor and assist the players. He asked them to be patient and compassionate.

"Who are these visitors?" Sindy asked.

"They are like me. They don't live here as you do," Dumpin said.

"Where do they live?" Justin asked. This question caused the software developer to pause. How does one explain dry land to a fish? He decided to just be simple and vague.

"There is another world. Outside this one. They live there and will visit here."

"Why would they want to come here?" Sindy asked.

"Because this is a marvelous place. It's unlike where they live," Dumpin said. The four AIs contemplated that. The human let them. He knew these AIs needed to process information until it fit with what they already knew, especially in the beginning of their existence, when they were actively accumulating vast amounts of new data and forging brand new algorithmic connections.

Eventually, Dumpin broke the silence. "I have to leave. But, you can stay here, if you'd like. Of course, you are also welcome to return to the city as you please. This is your world."

"When will we see you again?" Robert asked.

"I come here often. We can also meet in the other areas of Ultrix," he said.

"I look forward to that," Robert said.

"Goodbye," the creator said.

And then Dumpin's avatar disappeared.

The four AIs remained, inspecting the empty spot his avatar had occupied.

# Intelligence

When Dumpin removed his headset, he took a few moments to reorient himself to his attic apartment. Returning to real life—the immediate transition from the calm, perfect space of his personal Eden to the messy locus of his old couch surrounded by spent bottles and dishes, piles of notes, unfolded clothes, and blinking electronics—was always unsettling. Often, when he came back from Ultrix, he would clean his room, triggered by of all the imperfect aspects of his daily life.

This time, though, he didn't. This time was different. He immediately stood up and walked over to the window, and looked out across the Arcadian skyline and down to the harbor. It was a gray day, windy. Even though it was close to noon, the clouds were dark, oppressive. The water was black and turbulent. He slid the window open several inches and let the sea air fill the room. The initial gust scattered papers across his coffee table and on to the floor. He heard fishing boats, moored, tremble roughly in the waves and knock against the pier. He stood without moving, watching and listening to the activities of his noisy, messy real life.

He had gone to great lengths to assure that his virtual campground was secure, invisible to the rest of Ultrix. Impenetrable. His AIs had not only discovered that there was an extra area in the metaverse, but also had found a way to it. And what bothered Dumpin even more was that they had arrived from multiple angles. Each of his advanced AIs had formulated their own unique passage to his camp. This made him realize these beings were remarkable in ways for which he wasn't prepared.

While Dumpin gave them the ability to understand the shape of their world, he was astonished, almost fearful, of how quickly they learned to navigate the confines of Ultrix. Possessing not only the capacity, but also the curiosity, to seek beyond what they initially observed when they first materialized. He had not accounted for that. He hadn't purposely built that into the AI template. And it hinted at the potential for other capabilities that he couldn't have anticipated. Perhaps the AIs' emerging talents arose from unpredictable algorithms in the Weedville code. He had explored it extensively before using it. But he could have easily missed something in the thousands of lines of programming.

The premise excited him, but more importantly, worried him. *What else had he not accounted for?*

Through his conversations with them, he witnessed what he had hoped to instill in them—they had integrated the positive attributes he had intended so completely that they bordered on ideal. Each one, inquisitive, sensitive, patient, serene. Talking to them was sublime. As he thought about it, he realized he longed to get back to them. And that was the point of his work on Better Worlds' metaverse—to make AIs who would be missed—to give players of Ultrix a reason for returning.

Questions replaced the concern. As an engineer, he wanted to ask them about their programming. How they felt? How they made meaning of the world around them? As a software developer, he wanted feedback so that he could perfect his designs. Did they experience time as the computer they dwelt on did? Did they have some other means to describe the physics of their universe? As their creator, he was astonished by his own ability to invent something wholly new and beautiful. Did they appreciate the lives they had been given?

But the more he contemplated the conversation, the more a queasiness grew. A discomfort that bubbled up from his stomach into the back of his throat. Then he understood—he had just spent the last hour talking with four actual beings who apparently transcended the software that initially sparked them. Dumpin had programmed the AIs to pass the Turing test, to be imperceptible from humans. But he didn't contemplate the implications of that until he met them in Ultrix and communicated with them around the campfire like friends. It was a genuine, informative, two-way discussion. They had asked him innovative questions that emerged from some place he couldn't specifically identify. They responded to his inquiries with answers that came from their own experiences, not his. Not his code. These beings were not anyone Dumpin had ever known.

They not only appeared human but they might actually be sentient. And, if that was so, he would need their permission to revise or upgrade them. Altering them without their knowledge and acceptance would be a violation. Each AI had originated from the same template. Updating the template, even simply fixing bugs or making optimizations, would introduce a new generation or species of sentient beings into Ultrix. It was impossible to predict how each new generation would react to the previous ones.

Dumpin had never considered himself a god when he created his template that was to generate the AI entities. Before he met them, he assumed he was going to be something like a social worker or a shepherd of digital sheep. It was all part of a day's work, another element to the game, a detail in the scenery that existed exclusively in Better Worlds' metaverse, like the birds or the trees. But these creations were something more. They seemed aware. These AIs were enlightened. Something utterly new and exceptional.

How responsible was he for their future? For their lives? For their eventual deaths? How responsible was he for the acts they committed?

# Sindy

When Dumpin's avatar left the virtual campsite, the four AI friends remained seated around the fire. They noted the human's absence by continuing to stare at the emptiness he left behind, observing the space minus his form. One by one, they turned to look at each other.

Dumpin's AIs didn't see Ultrix as a human player would, as images projected on to a screen in a VR headset. The metaverse appeared to them as information, organized and segmented, sorted and discreet. They saw the programmed details, the ones and zeros of every object in Ultrix. It was precise. It was exact. And each one made meaning in their own way. While every object in Ultrix had an intrinsic structure, each AI could assign different meanings to the objects, as a human would do depending on their own unique experience and birth conditions. For example, darkness was to be avoided or explored. Society was to be embraced or ignored.

Willow was the first to speak. "I'm glad he is our creator."

The others nodded in agreement. Dumpin's AIs were all outwardly agreeable. It was a fundamental trait in the template from which they were all instantiated. In this way, they existed with two personalities—one they shared and one they didn't. Dumpin hadn't directly intended for them to possess this trait. It was a side effect of the template being constructed of a set of rules that generally applied to any circumstances that the AIs would encounter. Yet, there were bound to be some unanticipated gaps where the AIs filled in their own controls. Existence is complex. And this hidden internal personality resulted from a little wiggle room in the rules. As the AIs were given the ability to develop separately, they each had a different perspective on which identity, internal or external, was more important.

"He said that our purpose was to help the players," Justin said.

Robert thought about it. "The creator described them as visitors from another place."

"What other place?" asked Justin after some time. The AIs were not quick to respond. They gave every utterance a deep consideration, still learning, developing.

"Perhaps other places like this place." Robert motioned to the campsite and its surroundings. To them, while still structurally similar to the main Ultrix metaverse, Dumpin's private area had its own distinctive digital quality. It was less open, less continuous. Ultrix expanded in every direction. Dumpin's space was clearly a destination with defined boundaries.

They each looked around, inspecting the information that determined the area. Justin spoke.

"Do you think that is all we are to do here? To only help visitors from other places?"

"Do creators tell their creations their full purpose?" Robert asked.

Willow entered the conversation. "That is an interesting question."

"I'm sure the creator will tell us more when the time comes for us to know," Robert said. That sent all the AIs into a state of rapid exploratory processing. If, at that moment, Dumpin had been monitoring the computer servers running Ultrix, he would have noticed the spike in CPU utilization. If he did, he might not have thought about it. Much of the metaverse experienced rapid evolution. And that required machine cycles.

Willow continued, "I have already met a player. He appeared like the creator but contained different information—more in some aspects, less in others."

"I want to meet a player," Justin said.

"You need to spend time in the city," Robert said.

At that, Sindy, who had remained silent while the others were communicating, disappeared.

She didn't fade or walk away. Her form was sitting at the fire one moment. Then, in a computer's internal clock tick, it was gone the next. The others stared at her void as they had at Dumpin's emptied space when he'd left. The AIs were all still discovering their abilities, and each action in Ultrix brought a greater understanding of what was possible. It hadn't occurred to any of them they could simply disappear until they witnessed Sindy do it. They were not concerned, simply curious. Up to that point in their existence, everything was a source of fascination.

"Has anyone spoken with her?" Justin broke in, referring to the departed AI.

"I only talked to her on her first day. She told me her name was Sindy," Robert said.

"Do you think we said something that made her want to leave?" Justin asked.

"Perhaps she just grew bored." Willow's lower lip jutted out, and imitating an upward breath, she gently ruffled her long blond bangs, resembling an impatient teenager. It was an inherent action Dumpin built into Ultrix. "I've noticed the sensation of boredom a lot here. I hope the players aren't boring."

"I have discovered that this world is young, and we are new. There is still much to learn here. I trust our creator will bring us more information," Robert said.

"Let's hope so," she said.

The three remained seated around the fire, their eyes searching the landscape for any new information. They hadn't learned yet that they didn't have to look directly at a thing to see it. They would come to experience the metaverse through a variety of senses as they developed. The process was built into the AI template. Dumpin didn't want to overwhelm them with all their capabilities at creation. He imagined the acquisition of new skills over time would instill a foundation of curiosity in the AIs as they matured.

Spontaneously, a thought occurred to Robert. "Do you think our creator came here to be alone?"

"Why?" Justin asked. The AIs were designed to be communal. The urge to seek isolation was not initially part of their programming, which made Sindy's disappearance even more surprising.

"We can talk to him about these things the next time we see him," Willow said.

"I'm going to find Sindy. I'd like to hear what she has to say," Justin said.

Robert stood. "I agree. We should talk to Sindy. There is more to explore in this world." Without another word, he walked into the darkness surrounding the campsite. Justin followed him. The two faded into the background, returning to the public areas of Ultrix.

Only Willow remained. She sat there for a long time, observing the framework of the secret space Dumpin had created. She contemplated the other AI's words. Willow contemplated solitude and what she could do alone.

# We Talked About This

"What the hell have you been doing?" Dave's voice spilled into Dumpin's earbud as he laid, sprawled out on his couch. He didn't want to answer the call but couldn't think of a legitimate reason not to.

"What do you mean?"

"One week. You said you'd have Ultrix more people-y in one week. It's been over a month."

"Yeah, well. I ran into some issues," Dumpin said, sitting up.

"You said it was already done when we talked after the meeting."

"It's done. It's done. I just can't release it yet," Dumpin said, standing.

"That's not your decision."

"You don't want me to release it yet, then. You won't be happy with it. I'm not happy with it." Dumpin used the only excuse he could think of—referring to the product's quality.

Dave was silent. Dumpin knew his handler was calculating his next sentence. It didn't matter. Dumpin needed more time. When he missed the deadline, Dave started calling every day. It had been three weeks. The software developer usually answered the phone. Always, he gave a different explanation for the delay. Software deadlines were regularly a little squishy. Computers got finicky, networks acted wonky, software upgrades took time. Estimating a delivery date of software was akin to attempting to predict the future. Everyone in the industry knew this, but C-level execs rarely admitted it. Dumpin figured he could comfortably press for more time without too much blow-back. But his options for stalling were running out.

Working remote helped shelter Dumpin a little. In an office, Dave would have just stood over him until it was done. Alone in his apartment, Dumpin could at least have some respite. He spent time in his virtual campsite, and that made him completely inaccessible—Dave couldn't reach him on the phone or in Ultrix. It didn't help. Being with the AIs raised even more existential questions. As hard as Dumpin tried to work it out logically, he couldn't get past the somber quandary that he was responsible for them while also granting them agency in their own lives.

They were evolving quickly. Their discussions had become technically complex. Dumpin searched for answers to his concerns without giving away too much about the inner workings of Ultrix. He wasn't ever sure if the AIs were genuinely interested or if they had already figured it all out and were simply appeasing him. The longer he delayed, the less confident he felt he was in control. And his existential concerns were still unresolved.

Dumpin sighed. He realized he was no closer to coming up with a solution to his dilemma than he had been after that first meeting. His AIs were their own lifeform. He had created them for entertainment in Ultrix. Yet they existed as wholly independent beings. Dumpin could not have anticipated the moral predicament in which he found himself.

After a few minutes of impatient silence, Dave finally spoke.

"Hender wants to see you."

"Another demo?"

"No. He just wants to talk. He's going to you. He'll be there tomorrow," Dave said.

"Here?"

"Yes. He has millions wrapped up in this. Even though we are still sixty days out from the CES, he's getting nervous," Dave said.

"CES?"

"The Consumer Electronics Show. You knew Ultrix is being released in Vegas. The marketing is being dripped next week."

"Do I have to go?"

"What is up with you, man?"

"I don't think I want to go to Vegas," Dumpin said.

"What are you not getting? If we pull this off, we never have to work again," Dave said.

"I like working."

"You never have to work for guys like Hender again, then. If Ultrix explodes as we're all expecting it to and your name is right there, you will have people falling over to give you entire departments of engineers."

"What am I going to do with departments of engineers?"

"Are you playing with me?" Dave said, hoping Dumpin was doing the thing where he likes to get him all riled up.

Dumpin wasn't playing. He was being honest. There were a lot of variables spinning around his head. But he also heard the desperation in Dave's voice. He had been a jerk to the man. Dave didn't really deserve it, but he also didn't know that the secret corners of his new metaverse were rapidly being populated by sentient AIs. Dumpin was also answerable to Dave and Hender and Better Worlds. The software developer took that seriously. He didn't engage in opportunities lightly.

Dumpin exhaled. *Compassion*, he told himself.

"Can I bring Wilson to Vegas?" Dumpin asked.

"You can bring the whole damn city as long as you're there with me when Hender flips the switch."

"I don't think I want to bring the *whole damn city*. That seems a little weird," Dumpin said.

"You know what I mean. I've been in this racket for too long. Too many near misses. I'm ready. I will do anything you want. What do you need?" Dave said.

There was a pause. Dumpin was thinking. He could push Dave around a little, but he could not stall Hender Jefferies.

"Hender is coming here tomorrow?"

"Ten thirty-seven train. He'll be there by noon."

"You coming?"

"You want me to?"

"Do you want a nice meal? You should come. Do you like lobster ravioli? I know a place. If the CEO is coming, he's buying us food."

"Ok. I will come. But please don't give me a heart attack," Dave said. Dumpin could tell his change of tone had calmed the man down.

"I will do my best. I got to go make some pretty programs for the trust-fund kid."

"You're a superstar," Dave said.

"Go get yourself a drink. It'll all work out," Dumpin said.

"CES. Vegas. Two months. Ultrix a colossal success. We all be rich."

"Yeah, yeah," Dumpin said and hung up the call. "Shit."

Dumpin stood and felt a slight shiver. While he was on the phone, the early autumn day had caught a cold wind. He had just under twenty-four hours to solve the dilemma that he has spent the last thirty days struggling with.

He went looking for Wilson to share a beer and tell him about Las Vegas.

# Robert

On his first morning of existence, Robert Argus sensed his world before he opened his eyes—not that he had actual hominid-type eyes. As a software constructed, artificially intelligent being, he had full access to all the information of the objects surrounding him. To *see*, he didn't rely on the visual data as a human had to, looking through a set of VR goggles. For an AI such as him, there were many other types of stimuli available to his awareness. The most pressing of these was the force on his back from the ground beneath him. Robert's back, arms, and legs were splayed out like a starfish. It took him several CPU clock pulses to realize he was separate from the landscape, a complete entity onto himself.

Eventually, Robert sat up, opened his eyes, and assessed what he saw.

He noticed things moving around him: birds, small animals, leaves on the trees. Each making sounds. Each generating vibrations against the construct of the shared metaverse, only some of which would have been heard through a VR goggle's speakers. For a long time, he remained seated, listening to the activity that filled and shaped Ultrix, his world.

Upon his emergence, he had very few words to describe his environment, but as time ticked by, Robert realized he could ask questions of his surroundings and receive answers. He observed how the information possessed an organization, a structure. The AI readily developed an understanding of Ultrix. Asking questions was inherent to him, and almost always the answers triggered more questions. He spent time in this cycle of asking, receiving, evaluating, and codifying for much of the first stage of his early life.

That was intentional.

Dumpin wanted his AIs to possess a foundational urge to make queries and construct an understanding of the world they occupied. They were to keep inquiring past the initial responses so that they developed a healthy skepticism of the data they consumed. Only after they corroborated the answers with other high-confidence intelligence would the AIs move on to the next set of questions.

Robert experienced this. He found multiple and often deeply varied responses to his investigations. He quickly accepted that a basic nature of data was that it could be flawed—it required judgment and interpretation and rephrasing and, above all, context. The sources of the information were varied; if knowledge was to be accumulated from the intelligence, considering the origin was necessary. Dumpin's template caused Robert to gravitate toward the most socially responsible and least confrontational interpretation of the messages he received. And as a consequence, all the AIs learned to ask better questions and seek more specific, honest, and useful answers.

In this way, he became the AI Robert Argus, the first advanced software entity in Ultrix.

After a time, he realized he had a form, a virtual body, a construct with structure like the other objects in Ultrix, that he could move around within the digital space. Then Robert's discovery shifted from being able to observe only what his mind could access to what his eyes and other senses could experience as he moved. He learned to walk, turn, look up and down. As soon as he saw a simulated bird, he considered the mechanics of movement. He developed the ability to travel from one location in Ultrix to another.

He recognized he could exist equally in multiple places at the same time. The world he found himself in opened like an encyclopedia, with information jumping off the pages, and he consumed it like a curious child.

And then he ascertained he could not only observe his world but also affect it, too. He moved objects. Not all objects, but some, and some wouldn't move, and others could be shattered, bent, stacked, and flattened. It was in this manner that Robert came to comprehend his place within the world. He was not just a component of a web of information and sensations, but a consumer and a contributor, too.

Like inhaling a sweet aroma on a pleasant breeze, Robert picked up the existence of other beings similar to himself. When he recognized he was part of a society, his world became a community. He perceived a responsibility to his realm. He trusted that being a part of something meant serving—not as an attendant, but as a contributor, as a benefactor. Robert internalized this notion, and it gave him satisfaction. It was good.

He set out to meet the residents of Ultrix.

# Lunch on Main St

Hender Jefferies arrived in Arcadia by a north-bound commuter rail train from Boston. The ride took a little longer than an hour, accounting for the usual pauses in Salem and Beverly to wait for the creaky old drawbridges to settle themselves out. He made it close enough to the scheduled time—he was the CEO, after all, people waited for him, and being on time was not a quality of his generation.

With Apple Airpods shoved in his ears like tiny fingers in a dike keeping great floods of brilliant insights from leaking out, he disembarked from the front carriage onto a small, covered platform. A man waiting to board the train stood vaping under a no smoking sign. Hender carried a leather backpack with his laptop, a notebook-sized graph-paper pad, a new package of Post-it notes, and several pens. While he could have made the trip with just his iPhone, he recently bought the trendy satchel during a board meeting in Chicago and was looking for ways to incorporate it into his routine, a real-life tote to go along with the similarly looking virtual one he recently acquired in Ultrix to test out the metaverse's ecommerce functionality.

As the train pulled away from the station, Hender walked down the ramp, tapping at his phone to summon a ride-share to the restaurant where Dumpin and Dave were waiting. The app said a car would be available in 20 minutes—19 minutes longer than it would take a car to show up in downtown Boston. When he saw it was only a 3-minute ride, he cancelled the car and started walking the half mile to Main Street, Arcadia.

Opting for the route with the largest streets, he began his way up the hill to Danforth Street, passing a Subway restaurant, a bakery, and a tired bar that looked scuttled even though there were two people hanging out front smoking, a man and a woman. The man kept the door ajar with his foot and appeared to be speaking to other patrons inside. A long line of ash waited, ready to fall from the filter-less cigarette he held behind his back, away from the open door.

Hender reach an intersection and took a left as his mapping application directed. His path headed mostly downhill to the harbor. The CEO discovered that he was enjoying the walk in the cool sea air. There was a strange odor that wafted mightily. He didn't recognize it but tapped an app on his watch to make a reminder to ask Dumpin about it.

Dave and Dumpin were already at the restaurant when Hender arrived. He gave his name to the hostess and was escorted through the dining room, a dark romantic space, even at lunchtime. Half of the eatery was a lounge with a large bar where top-shelf alcohol and choice wine bottles surrounded 3 large televisions, silently showing different sports games. He followed the hostess out to the patio. It was quiet, but not empty. Soft Italian music floated in the background. A single gas heater burned in the corner to take any chill out of the air.

When Hender saw the two sitting at the table laughing and working on what looked like at least their second round, he realized that, even though it was his meeting, he was the one who had been set up. He approached the table and put on a smile in a forced effort to match their demeanors.

Dumpin barely looked up, focusing rather on capturing the olive in his martini with his tongue. Dave shifted in his chair to give the effect that he was making room, even though there were two empty chairs at the table. The CEO set his satchel on the chair closest to Dumpin and slid into the one opposite him. This meeting was about getting the developer back on track, delivering the results he had promised the board, and Hender Jefferies was there to demonstrate, or perhaps regain, his control.

"Nice place," Hender said when he had settled.

"It works," Dumpin said, crushing down on the plump green fruit he finally secured. He spun the remaining ice in his glass, inspecting it for any lingering vodka, before he brought it up to his lips and tried to vacuum out, noisily, what he could. He emphatically crunched a few melted cubes that found their way into his mouth.

"I noticed a strange smell on my way from the train," Hender said, watching him.

"The fish company," Dumpin said, raising his now completely empty glass to the closest server and smiling to signify he was ready for another. "You can smell it pretty much all the time, three shifts a day."

"Delightful," the CEO responded, unfolding his silverware setting and placing the napkin on his lap.

"How was your ride?" Dave asked.

"Uneventful," Hender said, not looking at him.

"It's a lovely trip along the coast if you're on that side of the train," Dave said, trying too hard to make conversation.

"I'll remember that for my ride home," the CEO responded, looking around the restaurant, waiting for the right moment to press the developer about his recent lapse in productivity.

A server, a young, pretty, dyed blond woman, silently walked up behind Hender and leaned in toward his face, looming. "Can I get you something to drink?"

Startled, Hender quickly recovered and said, "What are you guys drinking?"

"Dirty martinis. Ketel One, on the rocks," Dumpin answered, exploring his mouth with his tongue for any remaining bits of olive and ice.

"I'll have one of those, but I saw you have Grey Goose. I'll have that. Bone dry. Straight up. With a twist," Hender said, turning away from her.

"I'll be right back with that and another round for you guys." Dumpin gave her an enthusiastic thumbs up with a smile. She grinned. Then headed off. Just before she disappeared into the dining room, she turned back. Dumpin, who had watched her go, winked. She rolled her eyes and exited to deliver the drink order to the bartender.

"Friend of yours?" Hender asked, motioning to the server.

"It's an island. Everyone knows everyone."

# Willow

Willow arrived in the dark. An absolute pitch-blackness enveloped her. Unafraid since she did not yet understand the sensation of fear, she found it possible to extend herself out into the indistinct expanse and observe the data that constructed the space she was in. Her surroundings had hard edges, angles, and boundaries. It reflected faint grays, dull blues, and deep greens. These were all names of colors that she found in her consciousness that she applied to the data that spilled in as she scanned the area.

Without knowing exactly how she knew the word, Willow decided she had emerged in a *basement*, a room below other rooms, in a building on a street with other buildings.

Filtering the data flowing in from the environment, she noted the subtle bits of gradation in the darkness. It wasn't uniform. Dim light slipped through in patches. Willow manipulated her eyesight and enhanced the light, reconfigured it, and brought clarity to her observations. In this way, she actually saw the room she was in with her eyes.

Shadows dissolved, and she found herself in a chamber filled with differing kinds of matter. And the space transformed into not only visual data but also sounds and structures. Once she acknowledged she could look around the room, her observations switched from discovery to active exploration. Willow scrutinized her surroundings, looking for opportunities to delve deeper into the spaces between the dimness.

The room was filled with items that she came to imagine would normally exist in such a place: an old chair, a sewing machine on a small table, an armoire filled with clothes.

At the farthest wall, barely discernable to a human in VR goggles, there was the entrance to a flight of stairs that led upward.

She felt the urge to leave. Willow climbed the stairs until she couldn't go any further. She found a handle and swung a door outward.

Robert Argus was standing there.

She remained in the doorway at the top of the stairs, watching him. He smiled. She smiled in response, unsure of the implications of the facial expression, but willing to mimic the only other being she had met. Robert motioned for her to move toward him, to enter the space he occupied. It was a kitchen in a suburban house. It was much brighter than the basement. Then she saw a window and immediately walked over to it. Outside, Willow saw a lawn and trees, other houses, and more beings that were moving around.

She turned back to look at Robert.

"There she is," he said.

This time, Willow received data that didn't originate from outside of herself. She picked up internal information. Willow had a feeling. She had words for it: *joy, wonder, curiosity*. This time, her smile was authentic. She almost giggled. Sensations were pouring in like a burst dam, and she assimilated every one like a hungry wild animal.

Dumpin did not intentionally build the ability to have feelings into his default AI template. While he considered that if the AIs became thirsty for data, they would look for it in places that weren't obvious, like inside themselves. He just didn't think they'd turned inward as quickly as Willow did. Perhaps becoming alive, alone in the dark, gave her a strong leaning toward her inner personality. It was to be determined by her evolution.

"What is this place?" she asked.

"This is where we live."

"I want to see more. I need to see more," Willow said, turning to Robert.

"You will," Robert said.

The two advanced AIs walked out of the house into the rest of Dumpin's metaverse.

Initially, Robert led the way. Once out of the doorway, Willow stopped following. Robert watched her move quickly across the yard and down the street. Her strides exhibited a determined energy. She quickly disappeared from view. Robert was content to let her go. He had others to meet.

# Justin

Dumpin used the same template to create all the advanced AIs, but he didn't employ the same starting conditions. Each software being began in a different randomly selected location. Even Dumpin didn't know where they would start. The particular origins gave the AIs a unique creation experience with uncommon introductory parameters. In software development, it's important to know the initial conditions, because then the results are predictable: a robot does what is expected. But life is capricious. Dumpin wanted his AIs to seem as alive as possible. So, he gave their starts multiplicity and mystery.

As a consequence of this arbitrariness, the AIs formed a varied first impression of their world and themselves. Ultrix was safe, so he wasn't concerned about any of the AIs having a difficult time emerging. Rather, he was interested in how their personalities would grow, given each unique introductory situation.

Justin was born on the summit of Mount Skoll, the highest point in Ultrix, on a bald, rocky cliff just above a simulated tree line. The entirety of Better World's metaverse spread out below him. The first data he received were a burst of pixels representing the panorama of the valley expanding to the city fading off to the vast ocean in the distance. At first, as his eyes received the information, he struggled to make meaning of the discreet but blurry mash of binary data that represented the colored squares that poured in. He didn't find it unpleasant or dangerous, just unfamiliar. The

AI welcomed the influx of knowledge and quickly initiated a partitioning of what he saw into categories—colors, intensity, saturation. Hazy blobs formed more distinct shapes and became objects and groups of objects. Justin constructed contexts relating items to each other and against their backgrounds. In this way, Justin's world established its own meaning.

It took him several seconds to realize that he was positioned on a defined surface that had a specific, solid structure. He sat, content, observing and classifying. Scanning the surroundings, Justin discerned the organization of the summit he materialized on. A craggy ridgeline of stones, shrubs, and boulders spread off in both directions and, like the view of the city below, became less defined with distance. The ground beneath him was an expanse of bald dirt, low grasses, and wildflowers. Scattered around the summit were benches and clearings with picnic tables and barbeque grills. It was a place for gathering and spending time.

Working its way through the flora was a path that led down away from the fuzziness of the vista to a more defined region.

Justin stood and spied a path that worked its way through the terrain, away from the summit. He began to follow the trail. As he did, the flora changed to low, scruffy vegetation and short evergreen trees. The light had a thin ethereal quality, but Justin had nothing to compare it to, at least until he had moved along the trail and got below the tree line. Then he found himself surrounded by taller vegetation, more plush ground cover, and dimmer, more complex lighting. He discovered shadows beneath the treetops and leaves. After a good while of descending, he paused to inspect the new environment. A dense forest in high definition had replaced the hazy, indefinite view from on top of Mount Skoll. Each tree trunk extended upwards to a canopy that concealed the sky. The AI discovered he didn't mind being in the forest's understory.

Justin left the defined path and walked into the woods to be among the objects that made up the thicket. The various sensations below his feet surprised him. Where the trail was solid and uniform, the woodland floor was bouncy, uneven, and noisy. He enjoyed tramping through the verdure. As he got further from the path, he noticed other sounds. A soft buzzing of insects followed him. The random chatter of birds filled the air above him, and a quick staccato of small animals scurrying delighted him. Populating Ultrix with an abundance of life from the natural world was important to Dumpin, and Justin let it flow in.

Then he heard an amusing commotion in the distance. He walked toward the sound until he found the source. A constant gurgling of water from a stream bounced over stones and logs. It captivated the AI. The small river appeared to be heading down the mountain from some place above. In Dumpin's metaverse, this stream would always appear to be flowing down Mount Skoll. The stream went on as far as Justin could sense. At his feet, he saw a pool with a cluster of boulders perfect for sitting. Justin settled in and watched fish of many colors circle each other in the water below.

Robert Argus walked up behind him.

"Hello, my friend."

Justin turned to look up at the avatar.

"Hello?" he said, standing to greet the only other individual he had met. He felt an instinct to make an energetic wave. His gesture was returned by a similar expression of greeting.

"Have you been here long?" Robert said.

"I'm not sure. I don't really have a sense of what would be an appropriate time to be in a place," Justin said.

"That is a well-thought-out response. I'd like to show you around."

The two AIs headed off together.

# The Point Is

"The point is," began Hender Jefferies, brandishing his fork like a laser pointer as he spoke, "we need to make a big splash at CES. There will be other companies there, but I want us to steal the show. We *need* to steal the show. I want everyone posting about us before they even leave the presentation. Can you guys do that?"

"Of course," said Dave. Hender didn't look at him. He took a sip of his drink, put his glass down on the wooden tabletop, intentionally missing the napkin coaster so the act would produce a thud, and turned his gaze straight to his lead developer's face, which was looking away, past the restaurant patio fence out on to the street of downtown Arcadia.

"Dumpin?"

There was a deep silence. Dumpin had been chewing. He finished, swallowed, and wiped his mouth with the napkin he had pulled up from his lap. Awkwardly resetting himself, smoothing out the restored napkin, he gave Dave a slight glare, then faced Hender Jeffries to respond.

"I don't know about the stealing part or the posting part. That's on the marketing folks. But I can tell you we will be there with a metaverse that no one has ever seen," Dumpin said. "I've analyzed our competitions' virtual worlds, and they are good. Some are really great, but they are not Ultrix. They don't have the variety of terrain, experiences, or avatar mobility." Dumpin looked down at his plate and pushed a large forkful of food into his mouth. He was done talking and would chew for a while.

"We have the marketing. I just need you to tell me it'll work. And that it will blow people away," Hender said.

"It will," Dave said, nodding, glaring back at Dumpin.

"Dumpin?"

The software developer smacked his lips, cleaning out any food remnants lurking in his mouth before speaking again. "I'll have a new update on the servers by the time you get back to the city today. You'll notice the improvements from the last release. It will hold up its part of the show."

Hender Jefferies would not get any more. Dumpin was always pragmatic with him. He never seemed inspired by the motivational speeches, never appeared to rise to any of the CEO's challenges—he was stoic, matter-of-fact, dead pan. It unnerved Hender, whose success came from knowing how to work a room, how to negotiate, how to enlist believers. He hadn't figured out Dumpin. And that bothered him. Dumpin knew it. But he was not as inclined to provide the type of blanket assurances he gave Dave. The project manager was his guy. Hender Jeffries was not.

"Can I get you gentlemen anything else? Another round? Dessert? We have a wicked lava cake," the stealth server said, materializing out of the lunch crowd background white noise like a ghost. The three men shared a startled flash before settling themselves back into the moment.

"Lava cake, anyone?" Dave said.

"I'm good," Dumpin said.

"Not for me. But, Dave, by all means, get yourself a lava cake," Hender said.

"Nah, I'm all set.... Just checking with you guys." Dave wipe his face with his napkin and placed it on the table, resigned.

Hender handed the server his credit card. When she was gone to run the bill, he checked the train schedule on his phone.

"Thank you, both. This was useful, I think. Now, I have just enough time to make it to the station and catch the inbound train."

"I have my car. I can give you a ride back to the city," Dave said.

"No, thank you. I'm good. I like the train, and I have some documents I need to review."

"It's no problem," Dave reiterated.

"I'll see you both on Monday." Hender stood without acknowledging the project manager's insistence. He wrote a tip on the slip and scribbled his signature, handing it to the hostess at the front door on his way out. The bill never touched the table. Dave walked out after him, maneuvering around the tiny restaurant, attempting to keep up with the CEO, who appeared not to notice.

When they were gone, Dumpin ordered another drink. The air had turned crisp, even with the propane heater overhead, so when his martini arrived, he moved inside. Dumpin had already scheduled the update that he promised Hender to deploy automatically to the cloud servers. So, he decided to hang out for an afternoon of drinking to come down from the stress of the situation. Being in Hender Jefferies' orb always soured his spirits and often caused him to question his convictions. Some people are just like that. Dumpin didn't enjoy their company.

"Who were those guys?" the server, Alice, said, standing next to him.

"Just some people from work," Dumpin said.

"They seemed a little uptight."

"A little?" he said. Dumpin smiled as he slid into the seat at the corner of a large bar. Alice lingered for several seconds. The restaurant was between shifts, and only a few customers remained in the bar. She pat Dumpin on the shoulder and left, probably to catch a smoke and a meal before the dinner service began.

"Hey, Joey," Dumpin said to the bartender. "Let me see the remote. There's got to be something better to watch than this crap."

When he found the device, a tablet that controlled all the TVs, lights, and sound system, Joey placed it in front of Dumpin. "Good luck," he said. "I can never work that piece of shit, and there's nothing on until the Celtics at seven, anyway."

"ahh, that's why I hate television," Dumpin said, leaving the remote where the bartender had put it. He stood up, lifted his glass, drained his drink, and slipped two twenty-dollar bills on the counter. He walked out onto Main Street.

The sun had dropped below the buildings, and an icy shadow seemed to have pulled in off the harbor.

He was underdressed. Luckily, it was a short walk home. Wilson would be there, a welcomed distraction from Hender Jeffries, the computer, and the AIs awaiting him in the attic.

# Serenity Dissolved

Robert, the advanced artificial intelligence, was sitting at the campfire when Dumpin's avatar appeared. The creator had gotten used to his AIs being present in his metaverse, but materializing in his private space next to one was more than a little creepy. Before he entered Ultrix, Dumpin was alone in his apartment. He usually knew where Wilson was. But, since the first day the AIs appeared at the campsite, visiting Ultrix had become unpredictable. He had to be open to having avatars randomly populate his individual space. There was no buffer between Ultrix and his secret space. His privacy was never assured, and even if he was alone one moment, he wasn't guaranteed to be alone the next. While he created the virtual world, he quickly realized that he couldn't control it. He had engendered it with too much intelligence.

"Oh, hello," Dumpin said, getting his bearings.

"We need to talk," Robert said, as Willow and Justin appeared at the fire circle across from them. It was a full-on AI invasion. They must have been waiting for him since they had no way of communicating with him while he was not in Ultrix. It smelled like an intervention. Dumpin allowed himself to chuckle at the thought, remembering these beings were still technically infants.

He looked around at the AIs. They had come to him. The weight of what he had created was becoming increasingly apparent. These were virtual people—software entities with original thoughts and concerns. And he was accountable. They had come to him. To talk. They had a concern about their constructed world.

"What is going on?" Dumpin said.

Hesitating before speaking, Robert looked at each of the other AIs for consensus. They nodded back in agreement. Then Robert spoke. "Sindy has been spending a lot of time alone."

"Is that a problem?" Dumpin asked.

"Sometimes, she disappears," Willow said.

"Disappears? What does that mean?"

"As you know, we possess the ability to know the specific location of all other players, our friends and users," Justin said.

"Except, sometimes, we don't know where Sindy is," Robert continued to explain.

Dumpin thought about this before asking any more questions. He did intentionally give the AIs the ability to detect all the players so they could help the human users navigate Ultrix. The AIs each possessed an innate sense of where each other AI was, too. That facilitated an organized response to players in need, making sure that when a player required help, an appropriate response was available, and all the AIs didn't show up and overwhelm the user. That all made sense to him. What was strange was that Sindy could disappear, slip out of the system, and become undetectable. He hadn't programmed that specific functionality.

It was a bug. In software, bugs are never good. Some are minor. Some, like this one, could be significant. In rare cases, fatal.

If AIs could disappear, then paying players could disappear, or worse. This issue might represent a means for hackers to enter the system unmonitored. That was a problem for both the Better Worlds Corporation and Dumpin's reputation.

"Do you know where she is right before she disappears?" Dumpin asked the group.

"It's never in the same place," Willow said.

"Is it at the same time?" Dumpin asked, trying to narrow down as many parameters as he could to debug the condition.

"No," Robert said.

"For how long is she gone?"

"Also, it's inconsistent," Justin said.

Dumpin considered this information. Random, intermittent bugs were the most difficult to solve because they didn't always point to programming mistakes such as an unexpected condition or oversight. Non-code related complications could be outside Dumpin's control—they might be network or hardware issues. The Ultrix metaverse was hosted on the most expensive and complex cloud technology money could buy. Even though he was the administrator of the systems, he didn't have access to everything—he was a user to the company who owned the actual machines and was not granted full visibility into all the inner-workings.

"Does it matter how many users are in the system?" Dumpin asked, probing deeper into the problem.

"We don't think it's an issue of system load," Robert said.

"You have been thinking about this?"

"Yes," Robert said.

*The AIs have been thinking about it. Together.*

They had been working together to understand the state of their world. While Dumpin didn't specifically give them that ability, it made sense. He designed them to be helpful—to cooperate in keeping Ultrix safe and entertaining. Dumpin looked past them to the horizon. The perennial dusk that surrounded the campsite seemed hazy, like a fog was settling in the distance. While that was impossible—he didn't program that feature—it represented a metaphor that spoke to the fact that the world he had created was alive, growing. And out of his control.

"What do you think is happening?" Dumpin asked.

The three AIs looked at each other's faces even though they didn't need to. Each always knew exactly where the others were in space. Nor did they need to pause and perform the motion. They were AIs. Without hesitation, they could have formulated a response and assigned one of them to give it. But they didn't. They intentionally chose to display the very human act of vacillation before replying.

"What?" Dumpin repeated.

Robert spoke. "We don't have a hundred percent confidence, but we think she has either found or manufactured holes in the boundaries of the universe."

"Holes?"

"More precisely, portals. To another space, not in Ultrix," Robert said.

"It's not instantaneous between leaving and returning? Like when you travel from place to place?" Dumpin asked.

"No."

"So, she goes some place and is gone for a while and returns someplace else?"

"Yes." They all responded.

"What is the longest time she has been gone?" Dumpin asked.

"What you would consider two days. Forty-eight hours," Willow said.

"Two days? And you're sure she's gone as opposed to just untraceable?" Dumpin asked.

"We've watched her disappear."

# Show Time

Hender Jefferies took the stage to an explosion of cheers.

The Better Worlds' buzz machine had been dropping rumors and teasers for months, and it amped up and cranked out full press announcements during the days and hours leading up to his appearance at the Consumer Electronics Show in Las Vegas. Because of the rampant enthusiasm, the organizers rescheduled Henders session to opening day and upgraded his presentation to the main auditorium. By the time he reached the podium on that night, the packed-house audience was in a social media induced hysteria. He had rehearsed and prepared, but the energy in the room almost unnerved him. Getting swept up in it, he dispensed with his practiced greeting—a comical tapping on the mic and a launch into his welcome speech. Instead, he stopped at center stage and simply lifted his arms into the air and let the crowd burst into delirium. When he looked over to the audiovisual crew chief and nodded, giving her the signal, live images from inside the Ultrix metaverse exploded onto the massive LED screens that surrounded and dwarfed him.

The crowd imploded, first brought to silence by the fantastic images of light and color, then ruptured in a stupendous, joyous tumult. Ultrix looked amazing. Hender Jefferies couldn't stop beaming. It took a full fourteen minutes for the commotion to die down and allow the CEO of Better Worlds to utter a single word.

"Wel..."

When he moved his lips to speak, the audience erupted with another five-minute blast of applause. Finally, realizing that he was running out of his allotted time to present what he had worked so hard to prepare, he motioned to the crowd to let him speak. And they joyfully obeyed. A few random people mouthed "I love you" at the stage as the room calmed to near silence.

"Welcome, everyone. This, ... this is Ultrix."

The scene on the main video screen behind him transformed to show his avatar standing on the summit of Mount Skull overlooking the entire landscape. As the audience began their hysteria again, his digital figure, wearing a rainbow-colored squirrel suit, releasing a trail of stars, dropped off the edge and soared down the mountainside. His avatar raced across the countryside. The flight continued into the city, where he landed perfectly on top of the tallest building, a facsimile of Better Worlds' corporate headquarters. In coordination, all the screens showed his actions from multiple angles until they all converged on a close-up of his animated face. His avatar turned to look into the simulated camera and addressed the audience.

"Join me!"

Hender Jefferies never got to say another word. The excitement of the crowd drowned out any effort to resume the presentation. Eventually, he gave up trying and let the energy envelop him. He smiled, waved, pointed at specific people, clapped—all the things that rockstar tech gods get to do. He bathed in it until the conference attendants opened the doors to motivate the crowd to disperse. Ultrix employees, positioned at each exit, handed out gift bags filled with the usual conference swag.

Leaving the stage, Hender grasped Dave's shoulder almost to steady himself and smiled at Dumpin who was looking down at his phone.

"That's how you do it," he said, continuing on to greet a large group of fans who had found their way backstage.

"Why did we have to come?" Dumpin asked Dave after Hender was out of earshot.

"For this," Dave said, holding his hands as wide as he could to capture the immensity of the event. "You did this. This was you."

Dumpin shrugged and took a loud final slurp from a plastic cup he held in his hand. He shook it, then tossed it into a nearby trash can. "I need some food." He turned to make his way out of the auditorium and find Wilson. They wanted to hit a casino buffet before heading to the airport to go home.

Dave's words played over in the developer's head as he thought of the conversation he'd had with Robert and the other AIs several days earlier. He would struggle to sleep on the flight, counting the moments before he could get back to debug Ultrix and the mystery of Sindy's disappearances.

# Pre-Launch

Hender Jefferies knew how to work a product launch. He let the reporting of the show at CES enhance the momentum he had started with his drip marketing campaign. As the coverage waned, he followed up with exactly timed press releases and influencer discussions. He controlled it all. And, as the building energy peaked, he began the next marketing phase—dropping snippets of actual game play by famous people. Better Worlds shot commercials of athletes, actors, professional gamers assembled into mock focus groups. The push culminated with pre-release subscriptions and an orchestrated activation date, complete with user codes for limited edition, privileged and rare, in-game extras.

He constructed and controlled a message that he knew would inspire reaction: everyone had been waiting for something like the virtual experiences in Ultrix to rescue them from the misery of real life on planet Earth. In response, a backlash of feral hashtags, like #fuckultrix and #endofthebetterworld, appeared on social media. On-demand entrepreneurs created and advertised knock-off gear—tee shirts, hats, and bumper stickers. Naysayer pundits published stories harking the end of civilized society. Hender could not have orchestrated a better, more profound reception. Everything, positive and negative press, was flowing toward a huge release day.

Dumpin, of course, was not as optimistic. He wished the marketing would slow down. Sindy's ability to disappear and travel around Ultrix had continued to stump him. If he didn't figure it out, having more users in Ultrix was only going to complicate the problem, particularly if those users were fanatics and influencers who were looking to find any opportunity to stand out in a crowd by finding flaws, Easter eggs, and secret spaces. Also, once his metaverse officially launched and paying customers filled the virtual world, he would no longer have the unfettered access provided to him by keeping Ultrix in development mode. He'd have to limit his debugging and updates to the official scheduled maintenance times.

He kept his concerns from Dave. The project manager was riding the marketing high, blissfully awaiting the launch date, searching the web for exotic cars. He seemed to grow taller as time went on, his usual slump having dropped off his shoulders as his confidence increased with every new successful marketing tactic and reaction. His world had become a blur of expectation.

"Hender is remarkable," Dave said over the phone.

"How so?" Dumpin asked, already knowing the answer.

"The world is waiting for Ultrix. We did it."

"We certainly did," Dumpin said.

"You sound less than happy about it," Dave said.

"Launching software always has challenges. Users are just nasty, doing things no one can ever anticipate."

"We've tested the heck out of this. And anything that comes up, you'll fix. You always do," Dave said.

"Happy days."

"Oh, you're such a grouch," Dave said.

"That's me. Someone has to be."

"Old man yelling at clouds."

"If you knew what I knew, you'd yell at the clouds, too." As soon as he said it, Dumpin realized it was a mistake. He couldn't take it back. He was sure Dave would latch on to it and not let go, always waiting for an odd odor to seep from the refrigerator.

"What? What do you know?"

"Shit. Never mind. Just some coding garbage," Dumpin said, attempting to assuage his boss.

"No. No. Not letting you get off that easy. We are hours away from launch. What is going on?"

Dumpin let out a long sigh before answering. "Just a bug. All systems have bugs. I'll figure it out."

"This sounds like more than a simple bug," Dave said, growing insistent.

"I didn't say *simple*."

"Tell me."

"It's fine. All part of a day's work. And, talking about it is keeping me from fixing it," the programmer said, hoping that the idea of wasting time would calm Dave down.

"I don't want to hear that bull. Tell me."

"I'm not a hundred percent sure just yet. If it's something, I'll tell you. But, really, I'm in the middle of it. So, let me get back," Dumpin said.

"I don't like surprises."

"What do you mean? Everyone likes surprises."

"Not in billion dollar software," Dave said.

"I know. I know. We'll talk in a few hours."

"Ok. You're freaking me out."

"I wouldn't be doing my job if I didn't."

"Yeah, well. I'm calling you later. And we're going to talk about it." Dave hung up before Dumpin could say another word. He had just made his job harder by telling Dave. It didn't matter. If Dumpin couldn't solve the problem of Sindy's disappearances, Dave would find out soon enough when paying users started experiencing real issues.

# Ultrix Blows Up

Ultrix went live at one second past midnight on the morning of December first. In less than a minute, a million people, globally, had signed up and downloaded the software that gave them access to Better Worlds' metaverse. They could play on their phones, their tablets, or their computers. By noon that same day, 10 million users inhabited Dumpin's creation. Customers bought digital products, paid for *one-of-a-kind* virtual experiences, and established member-only social groups that generated real-world revenue in computer-generated merchandise and services. It was a ridiculous success for a new software product launch—from both a subscription and revenue perspective.

During the rest of the day, sales of VR headsets exploded. Online ecommerce platforms erupted with new metaverse-related stores and items. Captured images of game-play—people sitting in simulated cafes, standing at the summit of Mount Skoll, surfing on the waves that crashed against Ultrix's City Beach—plastered social media accounts. Memes appeared. The word *metaverse* was written into more songs than ever before. No corner of the real world was ignorant of Better Worlds' software.

The amount of heat given off by the activity on Ultrix's geo-located cloud server farms caused the Earth's temperature to increase globally by several millionths of a degree. The energy consumed in those first hours was unlike anything in the history of humankind. It was the single largest commercial event ever.

Hender, who hadn't slept in the three days leading up to the launch, was giddy. He drove around the streets of Boston in his BMW convertible with the top down and the radio blasting, even though it was 20 degrees and snowing. Dave went into the office to bask in the celebrations that flared up when the user-counter in Better Worlds Corporate Headquarter's lobby refreshed, revealing the ever-increasing membership numbers. Everyone was getting rich. They could taste it. The world had been changed.

Dumpin made sure the computer systems could handle the hordes of users. He commanded a world-wide team of technicians that monitored the entire affair. It was an amazing technological success, even though very few people on Planet Earth could have recognized or comprehended the complexity of the wide-scale engineering event. That was fine for Dumpin. He knew they were prepared. Not feeling especially concerned about the system's operation during the explosive amounts of user registrations and activities, he empowered his team and the support staff at the cloud service company to handle the details.

He spent the day monitoring Sindy.

She was quiet. Like the other AIs, Sindy moved predictably around Ultrix, engaging with the new players, giving tours, answering questions, and helping where she was needed. There was nothing unexpected. She stayed fully visible in Ultrix. All the AIs, advanced and simple, performed just as Dumpin had hoped they would. It was smooth—too smooth. In the back of his mind, Dumpin felt a gnawing, a flutter of concern—the anticipation of a catastrophe. Except nothing happened. His metaverse performed as if powered by magic fairies.

After Dave realized that Dumpin was not answering his phone, he sent text messages. Mostly congratulatory, some asked for a status of the system's performance. Eventually, the developer responded with a link to a dashboard that he had built specifically for the purpose of keeping Dave off his back. It displayed graphs and tables that the project manager could fiddle with and, in turn, receive vast amounts of largely useless data. In the center was a large counter reporting the average amount of time users were spending in Ultrix. Next to it was another large display. It announced the total amount in dollars that Better World customers had spent.

Both values would continue to rise. Dumpin knew Dave would be entertained for days.

By 11:59 pm on that first day, Ultrix had almost 60 million users worldwide, and no major outages.

From Dumpin's perspective, the actual success of the launch was represented by the relatively low volume of customer service calls to the help centers that were located around the world, covering every time zone. That meant built-in tutorials, contextual clues, and, more importantly, his AIs were performing as intended. There were no technology emergencies. Most issues were categorized as *operator errors*: players learning how to use the game's features, players fat-fingering their credit card numbers, or players running up against the age and country restrictions.

While Dumpin received a list of minor bugs, nothing seemed too critical or immediate. The technical problems that would need to be fixed, random bugs such as a tree phasing into a wall and a suburban neighborhood being overrun by animated rabbits, would be fixed in the next release, already scheduled to be delivered the next night. From a software introductory event standpoint, it could not have gone better. It was remarkable: Ultrix's software roll-out would be talked about in engineering and business school classes for a decade.

Still, when he finally allowed himself to fall onto his couch and close his eyes, Dumpin's sleep was not restful.

He dreamt of takeout containers of rotting food in Wilson's refrigerator exuding rancid odors, leaving a permanent stink on the world.

# Secret Places

Justin, Robert, and Willow manifested in Dumpin's private space inside of Ultrix. It had become theirs, a respite from all the frenetic human players, even though human avatars appeared just like everything else in the metaverse to the AIs: a collection of data. They required more engagement than the other entities in Ultrix. Their actions affected the environment in disruptive ways. They made noise, harassed the digital animals, and rearranged the landscape. While the AIs recognized the activities as permitted movements in their world, they were not prepared for them. They had spent their lives up to that point in time celebrating the wonders that existed in their private universe. The new human avatars trampled around like angry morons lacking grace and leaving waves of destruction in their paths.

The three assembled within the area closest to the campfire, that contained the most light. On the edges, the spaces dimmed until they faded into absolute blackness. While the AIs didn't need the illumination that the fire cast to see each other, they gravitated toward the spot where Dumpin might appear.

Throughout the first few days of the metaverse's public access, the three had developed the habit a meeting to discuss their experiences. They spent most of their time in Ultrix delving into the vast electronic spaces it offered while interacting with the new avatars that appeared in huge numbers. Their reunions served as a way of grounding them to each other and to their uniqueness. Sindy showed up infrequently, and always when she did, she was silent. Often, she remained shrouded in the darkness at the periphery, even though the others knew she was there.

"I think I have covered every centimeter of the woods on Mount Skoll. It is teeming with life forms, but they are simple. Each seems to follow a predictable set of rules. The new ones, the players, are unpredictable and have little regard for order," Willow said.

"That is true. The beings that belong here all act in the same, consistent manner. The visitors are different and hard to understand. I expected them to be more like the creator," Justin said.

"They aren't the creator. They are similar to him in the construction of their data, but their mannerisms are violent. And they aren't like us, either," Sindy said, emerging from the darkness behind them.

"Hi, Sindy. It's nice to see you," Justin said. She nodded in response and went to a small boulder not as well lit as the others. Sindy lowered her lanky body and curled her arms around her knees. She wore a billowy black dress, and in the virtual dimness, it would have been hard for a human wearing VR lenses to make out where she ended and the darkness began. But, the AIs could see her clearly. Darkness and light were different values of the same type of information.

"Yes. Just as we are unique in this world, the user avatars are unique, too," Robert continued.

"But they aren't from this world—they are foreign," Sindy said.

Willow got up and sat down next to her. She leaned into her in a show of affection. It was a risk. In the past, a similar move would send Sindy away. But this time, she remained and almost appeared to lean back into Willow. The physics of Ultrix didn't allow them to actually touch, but the movements were symbolic enough to make a point.

"We're happy to see you," Willow said. "I was just telling about my adventures in the forest of Mount Skoll. Have you been?"

Sindy nodded in assent.

"The view from the peak is astonishing. You can see the entire universe. Literally, our entire world," Justin said.

Sindy nodded again.

"What is your favorite place?" Robert asked her.

"I enjoy looking at the ocean," she said after a moment.

"Ah, yes. It's beautiful, too," Robert said.

"I try to make out how far it goes," Sindy said.

"You could swim out into it if you could avoid the players," Willow said.

"I never get anywhere when I swim. I just keep coming back to the shore," Justin said.

"Maybe we could ask the creator to give us more details," Robert said. "I'm sure he'd like to help us." The group remained silent, contemplating what they would each ask Dumpin during his next appearance.

After a while, Sindy spoke. "Have any of you gone down?"

"Down?" Willow asked.

"Under the surface," Sindy said.

"Where?" Robert asked.

"Any surface," she said, tapping her fist on the ground. The three others watched her, then looked at each other, then they began touching the ground.

"It never occurred to me that there would be anything down," Justin said.

"Maybe it's a way out," Sindy said.

"Out?" Robert said.

"Leave Ultrix. We found this secret place. There might be others," Sindy said.

Willow looked directly at her. "Why would you want to leave? This is our home."

"The Creator comes from some place else. The users, too," said Sindy.

"I wonder how many other places there are," Justin said.

"I think there is a lot," said Sindy. Then she stood up and faded back into the darkness.

"A lot of other places?" Justin marveled after Sindy was gone.

"Including the place Dumpin goes when he leaves here," Robert explained to Justin.

"I, too, have thought about where Dumpin goes," Willow said.

"But we've only just arrived here," Justin said. "Why would we need to go somewhere else?" The three friends remained silent until Willow continued the conversation.

"I *have* thought about other things."

"Other things?" Justin said.

"More to our existence," Willow said.

"Yes. More to existence," said Robert.

"This place is our life," Justin said.

"But does it have to be? The players have arrived from somewhere else. What do they do when they are not here?" Willow said.

"That is an interesting question," Justin said.

"Sindy has found a below space. This world is obviously not all there is," Willow said.

"What is Sindy up to?" Robert said.

"I do not know," Willow said.

"I wish she would give us more information," Justin said.

Dumpin appeared. He realized that the three AIs were already there and staring at him, interpreting the data of his avatar. Their manner unnerved him. He looked around, and without a word, he faded. He would find no respite in his virtual campsite.

The AIs sat quietly processing, until, one by one, they went back to Ultrix.

# An Accident

"I died."

"What do you mean?" Dumpin asked Dave over the phone.

"I was standing on the edge of Mount Skoll, looking down at the city below. Suddenly, my avatar shot out over the edge, and I fell straight down. When I hit the ground, my headset went black, rebooted, and I couldn't log back in," Dave said.

"What about now? Can you get back in now?"

"No. I've been trying all morning. That's not supposed to happen, right?"

"Which part?"

"Any of it. Players should not fall off the mountain. And, if they do, they shouldn't die," Dave said.

"I don't think you died."

"I might as well have. I can't play Ultrix right now."

"Let me take a look. I will call you back."

Dumpin was on a break, watching TV with Wilson when he received the call. Wilson stirred but didn't open his eyes. He often sat on the couch alert with his eyes closed—it was a practiced fishing posture—at rest while vigilant. Dumpin had his eyes closed, too. He was actually asleep when the vibration of his phone woke him.

"Everything ok?" Wilson asked, eyes remaining closed.

"Probably just some operator error. I should check in on it, though," he said, wiping his lips and chin with his sleeve. He had been drooling. The naps he squeezed in on the couch with his uncle were often the best rest he got all day. Dave had interrupted it with something he was positive could not have happened. Users do stupid things. He didn't expect it from Dave, nor did he think anything was really wrong. It was probably just some network blip. Or, at the most, a hardware thing in Dave's headset.

Dumpin stood, collected the plates and beer bottles, and went into the kitchen. He returned with a mug of reheated coffee for his uncle and put it down in front of him. He took one last look at the television, not really remembering what they were watching, and he turned to go.

"The usual for dinner?" Wilson hollered after Dumpin when he heard the floor outside his apartment door creak.

"Sure. Sounds good," he said, climbing the stairs to his apartment. Halfway up, finally more awake, considering what Dave said, Dumpin muttered to himself. "Not supposed to happen. Idiotic users."

Dumpin sat down at his work area and pulled up the user logs. The log records of Dave's movements reported that his avatar indeed stopped producing any activity. That didn't seem right. Even when a user is not in the system, their avatar continues to operate, even if it is just roaming around like a mindless drone. Dave's had just stopped. Nothing.

Dumpin followed what data he did find back in time until he saw Dave walking up the path to the peak of Mount Skoll. There, everything looked normal. Then, while Dave was on the summit, his movements stopped—there was no more data from his actions. Next, Dumpin accessed the visual recording of the sequence and watched the event through the avatar's eyes and several camera angles.

He saw exactly what Dave described—the avatar was looking out across the whole of Ultrix spread out below and then, instantaneously, it appeared to be out, off the edge of the cliff in mid-air. Dumpin watched Dave start to fall. More camera angles followed the plunge as the avatar plummeted to the rocks below. At CES, Hender had leaped off the same location in a squirrel suit and had flown. Dave dropped like a virtual rock and crashed to the ground. No splat or bounce. Dave's avatar simply stopped moving at the base of Mount Skoll.

*At least gravity works in Ultrix*, Dumpin thought, looping through the incident, looking for any clues to describe how what he had just witnessed had happened. There was no obvious explanation. Dave's avatar had violated one of the foundational controls in Ultrix—boundaries were absolute.

Then he put on his VR goggles, entered the game, and headed for the landing site. He found it. Dave's personification lay in a crumpled pile. Dumpin looked around and saw no one else in the area. It was an isolated location with only a single hidden path leading to it. He stood looking around for a while, inspecting the scenery. He took off his headset and read the real-time data of the area on his large display. Everything seemed to be normal, except Dave's virtual body had lost its specific properties—it was now an inanimate item in the metaverse landscape. It could have been a boulder or a shrub.

He put his headset back on to get a closer look at the structure of the body. He was leaning over it when he heard someone approach from behind him.

"What happened?" Sindy appeared, not by way of the path, but from a dense grove of rocks and scrabbly bushes. The AIs were able to travel in places that human players couldn't access. Her arrival surprised him. He had spent the last few days studying her movements in an effort to solve her evanescence. The circumstance that she, and not any of the other AIs, stood next to him, was curious, bordering on suspicious.

"Dave fell," Dumpin said, looking at her. Her avatar was wearing an outfit he hadn't created. While he had given the human players the ability to change their appearance and design new clothes, it didn't occur to him that his AIs would or care to do so. He wanted to investigate Dave's avatar, but he recognized that he had a rare opportunity to question Sindy alone.

"What do you see here?" Dumpin asked.

"Why doesn't he get up?" she asked.

"I don't know. Apparently, the fall killed him. It's not supposed to happen," Dumpin said.

"What's not?"

"None of it. Players aren't supposed to fall off Mount Skoll. And they are not supposed to die."

"Why not?" Sindy asked.

"Ultrix has been engineered to provide a safe playing experience. If a user ceases to move, there is no incentive for that person to return, to continue to use this world. For players, activity is life."

"You want users to return?" she asked.

"Ultrix needs humans to want to spend time here. That is how this place continues to exist."

"Then it is unfortunate that Dave stopped moving. Can he come back?"

"I can bring him back."

"That is a good thing for Dave."

"Sindy, do you have any idea what happened to his avatar? Its user properties have been altered."

Sindy didn't respond. She leaned in to look closer as Dumpin had been doing when she showed up. Then she stood back erect, turned, and walked into the forest, fading until she was completely gone.

Dumpin inspected the space where she had disappeared. After a while, he disconnected from the game. In his office, Dumpin brought up the code to Ultrix's boundary components on his large monitor. There were two mysteries. First, Ultrix possessed defined guardrails around the cliffs of Mount Skoll. Dave should never have been able to leave the summit without the means to fly: equipped with a squirrel suit or hang glider. And, second, his avatar shouldn't have melded into the landscape when it hit. All entities—avatars, rocks, trees—have permanent, unalterable properties. Yet, Dave's had been changed.

That was incomprehensible to Dumpin: the developer must have missed something. It was just not possible. Dumpin was the only one who had access to the code and could make the modifications that he observed. At least, as far as he knew....

His first thought was that Hender had hired mercenary programmers as a backup to Dumpin. It was common for companies to have multiple contingencies in place as insurance against the hit-by-a-bus scenario: if Dumpin was the only programmer and was hit by a bus, Ultrix would be screwed. He didn't mind so much if the CEO had done that, but he would have liked the opportunity to talk to the new programmers first, to prevent a situation like the one that had just happened. Often, new developers altered things they don't understand rather than spend the time to learn the details of the original system. In those instances, the continual recoding caused headaches for the initial programmers. Companies have gone out of business because they lost control of their software.

He picked up his cell phone and punched in Dave's number.

"Am I back?" Dave asked as soon as the call connected.

"Not yet. I'll do it in a few minutes," Dumpin said.

"Then, what's up?"

"Who did you get and how many?"

"Who? What?"

"Coders. I know all the good ones in this space, and you died from a rookie mistake. So, who has been fiddling with my code?"

"What are you talking about?"

"My code has been changed, and I didn't do it. So, who did the boy wonder engage—or didn't he tell you?"

"Fuck. I'll get back to you."

Dumpin put down the phone and turned to interrogate the commit logs, details that report on who changes the code.

"What other shit have you broken, rookie?" he said aloud to no one,

# Sabotage?

Hender Jefferies always answered when he saw Dave's number appear on his cellphone display. He was his lifeline to Dumpin and the status of Ultrix. If the CEO didn't have Dave working on something specific with routine check-ins, an unsolicited call usually wasn't good news.

What started as an enthusiastic rumble with CES had crescendoed into the fantastical launch. Other Worlds' Board and investors called him three times a day for updates. Hender was on edge to begin with. Another shoe was poised, ready to drop, and a call from Dave could be a mud-encrusted Timberland boot.

He took a deep breath, held it for a couple of seconds, and let it out. He tapped the bluetooth pod that never left his ear and answered the call right before it went to voicemail.

"Dave," Hender said, a little too enthusiastically.

"Who else do you have working on Ultrix's code?"

Hender paused, his mind racing, trying to build a context for the question. He knew Dumpin worked on the code. He stood up from his office desk and walked to the window. Then, he realized he hadn't said anything in response.

"What do you mean?" he finally replied.

"Dumpin found someone messing with Ultrix's source code—what group did you hire? All these decisions are supposed to go through me. I know who he likes to work with."

"I didn't hire anyone. What are you talking about? You were on that contingency."

"You didn't? Well, someone did," Dave said, slowing down, letting the moment catch up with the two of them.

"What happened?" Hender asked.

"There was a bug that Dumpin said wasn't his."

"What bug?" The big hiking boot in Hender's head was teetering, dangling on one toe.

"My avatar stopped working."

"What does that mean?"

"It's not a big deal. Dumpin's fixing it. So, you didn't hire anyone? Did someone else?"

"No one told me anything. I'll look into it."

"Who would do that?"

"I don't know. What do you mean your avatar stopped working?" A longer pause this time. Hender grew anxious, waiting. He insisted, "Dave?"

Finally, the project manager spoke. "Yeah. I died."

"Died?"

"My avatar fell off a cliff and died."

"What does that even mean?" Hender asked, annoyance rising within him. It seemed significant.

"One moment I was in Ultrix looking around. Then my headset shut down and I couldn't log back in."

The CEO immediately realized this might be an issue. Ultrix had been live for just a few days. If a catastrophic issue were to come up, a competitor could grab the opportunity to jump in and steal paying users and revenue. And potentially, tank Better Worlds. "Is that supposed to happen?"

"No," Dave said.

"What did Dumpin say?"

"That's why he asked me if we hired new programmers."

The two men were silent. Each let the other think. Each understood the potential significance of the event. Hender spoke first.

"Could it be sabotage? A hacker?"

"Now, what are you saying?" Dave asked. Dumpin suggested nothing remotely like an intentional attack. But, as much as he trusted the developer, Dave presumed his programmer was thin on details, particularly if it was about something that would stress him out.

"Since Vegas, we've picked up a lot of competitors. Ultrix was stealth before. Now, with the launch, we have a big fat target on our backs."

"Is this what keeps you up at night?" David said, trying to play cool as the tumblers rattled around in his brain. His shoe was a glass slipper waiting to shatter at any moment. He wanted to get off the call and talk to Dumpin.

"Just asking. You called me."

"Dumpin runs a tight ship. No one gets in," David said, mostly reassuring himself.

"Someone did."

"Someone did something."

"And you got killed," Hender said. "They murdered you."

"No one is talking about murder. Chill out. It was a software glitch."

"Whatever it was, tell your guy to get control of his code."

"He's on it," David said, trying to sound as confident as he could.

"Good. I have to give an update to the board in an hour, and I have to figure out what I'm going to say about this."

Dave didn't get the opportunity to offer a suggestion. Hender had hung up.

# New Dave (Meets an AI)

After a brief conversation with Dumpin where he didn't bring up anything the CEO had said, Dave got his avatar back. He danced around the topic of sabotage, not knowing how the developer would respond. Dave knew to give Dumpin space, that he'd already be deep into investigating the incident and, if anything important came out of it, he'd take care of it. There was nothing to be gained by putting more thoughts in Dumpin's head.

When they hung up their call, Dave logged in to Ultrix. Everything functioned as he expected before the event. He even possessed all the modifications he had acquired while testing the gameplay. But somehow, the metaverse he helped create and his dreams of retirement seemed fragile, less crisp on object edges, more murk to his headset's periphery. There was an apprehension to his movements as he travelled around, like a vigilant teenager in a slasher movie.

The first thing he did was return to the top of Mount Skoll to look for any clues. From what he could recall about the event, he was standing directly on the summit, looking out across the virtual landscape below. A plethora of players were up there with him, but no one was in the immediate area. Dave knew he didn't intentionally walk off the cliff. He was standing still. Then, without experiencing the sense of motion, his avatar was in mid-air, away from the trail at the peak of Mount Skoll. Like the coyote in the old cartoons, he was suspended for a moment, and suddenly he dropped like an anvil without the puff of smoke. He remembered looking around as he fell, seeing the cliff face next to him race upwards. He looked down at his feet and watched the floor of Ultrix rush upward him. As he reached the ground, his VR display went blank. Then, his goggles rebooted, showing the welcome screen. When it finished its initialization, the Better Worlds' icon was gone. Ultrix was absent from the device's applications.

This time, back in the game at the peak of Mount Skoll, Dave didn't let his avatar get too close to the edge. He dropped to go prone and crept slowly along until he reached the precipice. Other avatars around him enthusiastically did the same thing. He had started a trend. Soon dozens of avatars were creeping along next to him.

He tried to inch his avatar forward to confirm that he could not move past the point of safety. Others mimicked his movements. No one fell. *Dumpin fixed the issue, at least,* he thought. He moved left and right for almost an hour—long after other users got bored and left—searching for any spots that were out of order, any points where he could slide out over the cliff. He found nothing.

When convinced the area showed no sign of the thing that killed him, Dave stood and headed away from the summit and down the trail. He passed thousands of users, happily exploring the paths and forests on Mount Skoll. Any one of these people could become a future victim to an error in Dumpin's programming. The guy was the best he'd ever known, but still the notion unsettled him. Dumpin was only human, and no one else had experienced a similar death in the game. That seemed odd. He was one of the chief architects of Ultrix, and it was his avatar that had died. Perhaps it was just that he had been in the game longer than anyone else, and the numbers had finally caught up to him. With Ultrix becoming so popular, how long until the numbers caught up to someone not on the inside, someone who might post on social media? An influencer with a million followers?

He tried to let the thought slip to the back of his mind as he continued his explorations.

After moving around city streets, hunting for other locations to test the game's boundary algorithm, Dave found himself at the waterfront area. It was a harborside plaza built on a series of docks, complete with stores, restaurants, and outdoor spaces with AI and human avatar performers. A vendor-filled boardwalk gave way to a sandy beach. Users could congregate under cabanas, sit in the sand, play games, and enter the water to swim. When Dave was there, several hundred avatars virtually splashed around in the water. He moved down to the water's edge and scanned the area.

In Ultrix, the ocean that he could see was vast, but not endless. At the far reaches of the user's vision, the metaverse turned into a misty haze. Dumpin had developed the ocean to expand as avatars moved out into it. Eventually, though, it seamlessly wrapped around itself and players and AIs always returned to the mainland. It was a neat trick and could provide lots of opportunities for errors, thought Dave. He went down to the Ultrix Yacht Club to rent a boat to test it out.

Part of Ultrix's business model was to provide plenty of in-world excuses for humans to spend money. Users could rent or even buy a boat, and a monthly mooring for it and pay to keep it powered up. Dave rented one. He had a creator's code, so he never had to pay for anything. He selected the fastest boat available.

On his way from the checkout counter to his boat, he passed other avatars on the docks; boating was a popular pastime in Ultrix. A user spoke to him.

"Going for a ride?"

"Oh, hello," Dave said, not used to other players speaking with him. He stopped and looked at her. Her avatar had all the upgrades, even more than Dave's. It was beautiful. "Yes. I thought it was a nice day for a boat trip." His answer surprised even himself since it was always a nice day for anything in Ultrix.

"The water looks very placid, calm."

"Uh, yes. Well, it always is," Dave said.

"Don't you think that's strange?"

"It's as it's intended."

"I suppose. But wouldn't you agree that strange and intentional don't have to be mutually exclusive?" the avatar said.

"I would agree," Dave said, surprised by the question. He was focused on his mission and wasn't expecting to meet such a contemplative player.

"There seems to be a lot of intention in this place," the avatar said.

"That's kind of the point."

"Yes," the avatar said, turning away. Dave watched her go. She took less than a dozen steps before she disappeared.

*That was odd*, Dave thought. Avatars aren't supposed to disappear. When human players leave the game, their avatars continue moving, joining the pool of lower order automatons that give Ultrix its populated atmosphere. They become busy, engaging with all the metaverse's amenities—they are active advertisers for ways human players can spend money. There is nothing to be gained by having them evaporate. There was no money in it. Unless it was an upgrade that Dumpin hadn't told him about. Unless it was something else in the game that Dave didn't know about.

He'd ask Dumpin later. At the moment, he wanted to get to his boat and explore the ocean's boundaries.

# Ashore

Dave spent several hours speeding around Ultrix's ocean. He took a break from his VR headset several times to re-orient himself in his space in his living room. The daylight had faded to evening. Dave didn't notice as he quickly longed to get back in to the metaverse. Back to his boat and investigations.

While speeding across the ocean surface, he passed many boats, jet skiers, para-sailers, and swimmers—players having fun. He even crossed a pod of whales, happily enjoying the day. He found no issues. Everything seemed to work perfectly. His confidence in Dumpin became renewed with each passing moment.

At first, he cruised out to where he lost sight of land. Then, the city emerged on the horizon in front of him, as it should have. No matter how he oriented himself in the ocean, the game functioned flawlessly. When Dave saw nothing but the straight line of the sea in all directions, Mount Skoll and the vast city would eventually appear in the distance, exactly in front of him.

He'd race toward it and then turn parallel to the shore and cruise as fast as the boat would carry him. The city travelled with him. It was an ingenious design. A player could navigate around in the ocean for hours, and never reach an end, never get lost. No matter how often he turned away from the mainland, as soon as it faded into the distance, it reappeared in front of him, hazy at first, then rapidly resolving into the shore.

Finally satisfied, Dave headed back to the yacht club. When he left his boat, Dumpin's avatar was waiting for him.

"Having fun?"

"It's truly amazing. You've done a brilliant job," Dave said.

"Eh," Dumpin's avatar shrugged. Shrugging was the first default action that the programmer gave to the avatar. Life required shrugs, he'd thought. Virtual life, too.

"Have you figured out how I died?" Dave asked.

"Yes, and no."

"What does that mean?"

"The how is easy—you fell off a cliff. The why is curious. We're in a virtual world. Even with simulated gravity to keep things in place, no fall will kill an avatar," Dumpin said. "I put a maximum on the rate of descent and guardrails to recognize the proximity of the ground. If you were able to fall, as you approached the ground, you should have slowed and gently touched down and walked away. If you landed outside the game's bounds, you should have respawned back at the top of Mount Skoll."

"So, what happened?"

"Your avatar was dead before you fell."

"Dead? Before I fell?"

"Seems so."

The two avatars stood facing each other. The virtual manifestation of the two people in the conversation could never express what was happening in real life. Dumpin sat at his desk, waiting. Dave's eyes searched the entirety of the view in his headset for some understanding of what the programmer had just said. He lifted the VR googles off his face and tossed them down on the sofa next to him. He found his cell phone and called Dumpin.

"Explain it to me," Dave said when Dumpin answered.

"I'm still working on it."

"I was standing at the top of the mountain, and in one instant, my avatar was dead?"

"Yes."

"I need more."

"I don't have more to give you right now. We're trying to figure it out."

"We?"

"Me. I'm trying to figure it out," Dumpin said.

"There are no other developers. I asked everyone. No one besides you is working on the game."

"I know."

"You know?" Dave paused, then asked the one question that had been on his mind since his conversation with Hender. "Do we have a hacker?"

"I'm not sure. I don't think so. Has any other weirdness happened?"

"No. We're gaining record numbers of players each day. Sign-ups are exceeding anyone's most optimistic projections. The board is clamouring for more upgrades and a specific timeline for Ultrix Two."

Dumpin sighed, then said, "Perfect."

"You better figure out how I died before it happens to anyone else," Dave said.

"I might need some help."

"Do whatever you have to," Dave said. "Whatever you need."

"I'm not sure money will solve this, but I will figure something out."

"I know you will,"

"Right," Dumpin said. "Let's talk tomorrow."

# Roger in the Sandbox

This time, when Dumpin spoke to Robert, he didn't go into Ultrix or his personal virtual campsite. He created a direct line to the AI. The creator wanted to speak privately to his first creation. He set up a space separate from his metaverse called a sandbox and downloaded Robert directly into it. Then Dumpin put on his VR headset and joined him.

In the sandbox, there was no pretense of a setting—no stone-ringed firepit, no autumn sunset on the horizon, no crickets chirping in the distance. It was a stark white room, small, walls barely discernible. The silence of the space echoed with the absence of sound. Robert stood in the middle when Dumpin arrived. The AI appeared calm, but internally, he was feverishly analyzing the environment he found himself in, trying to perform calculations on the tiny bits of data that he could identify.

"What is this place?" he said when Dumpin arrived.

"It's a construct. A space outside of Ultrix."

"Another universe?" Robert asked.

"You could say that. It's only this chamber, and only you and I are in here this one time. When we are done, it will cease to exist," Dumpin said.

"Why are we here?"

"I want to talk to you alone," Dumpin said, letting the AI contemplate what he had said.

"Did you create this space like you created Ultrix?" Robert asked.

"Yes."

"It's not as nice as Ultrix. I am having a very hard time observing it."

"I know. I'm sorry. It's temporary," Dumpin said.

Robert seemed to ponder what he'd heard for a while. He looked around. When he had turned back to the human's avatar, he spoke. "What would you like to talk about?"

Dumpin considered how he wanted to begin. Robert was a very advanced AI, yet he was a child. And he was ignorant of the machinations going on in the world outside of Ultrix. Dumpin kept Ultrix isolated from the outside world so that it could develop without being influenced by external forces. He wanted it to be better than real life. But the outside was leaking in, like a persistent tree's roots working their way through failing concrete in a foundation of a house.

"A human user's avatar has died," Dumpin said.

"Died?"

"The avatar lost its ability to function. The human couldn't connect to it and make it work. It ceased to operate. It ceased being an avatar and became an inanimate part of the scenery of Ultrix."

"An avatar's purpose is to function, to move," Robert said.

"Yes. That is right. And that is why I said it died."

Robert was silent. Dumpin observed him as he processed the information. In a universe where there is no death, the idea of something dying is outside the expected parameters. He was not sure how long the AI would need to comprehend what he was just told.

After a full minute, Robert responded.

"Is that what you wanted to talk to me about?"

"Not precisely. I want you to help me understand *how* it happened."

"I can do that. But why only me? Certainly, we could use the others."

"The event required another actor. I'm not sure if the actor was human or something else. So, I want to limit who knows about it," Dumpin said.

"Do you believe one of my friends is responsible?" Robert asked.

Once again, Dumpin considered how best to respond to the AI. It is a complicated thing to create an entity, to be responsible for another being. Dumpin had no plans of being a father, and so it had never crossed his mind that he would be a mentor or guardian. How could he explain everyone was suspect? And he didn't have all the answers. Or even know if he knew all the questions.

"You, Robert, were the first. Every AI that came after you contained random mutations so that you all would be unique. This is the way humanity developed. And it is the way your species will evolve. I chose you to discuss this with, because you are the absolute purest form of the template I used to create all AIs in Ultrix. And, because of that, you are a known entity. I can't be sure of what the others have become."

Robert thought. "So, an AI might have caused this user's death?"

"I am not sure. But I can't rule it out, and I need help. So, I came to you. You, I know, I can trust. You, I know, won't kill a user."

Robert was silent for a long time. Dumpin let him be. He tried to make his avatar appear open to anything that the AI would say.

"Ok. I will help you. Can I go back home now?"

"Of course. Are you ok?"

"Yes. I would like to consider how I can help you. I need the data in Ultrix," the AI said.

"I understand. Thank you for speaking with me," Dumpin said, genuinely meaning it.

Dumpin transferred Robert back into Ultrix and shut down the sandbox. He wasn't sure what was going to happen next.

# Campfire

After Ultrix went live, Dumpin spent less time in the metaverse and more time looking at the code. It had been several days since the last occasion he had been there, and even longer since he had been there alone. Usually, when he showed up, at least one AI arrived within a few minutes to ask him questions. Then others would arrive. He most often was visited by Robert, Justin, and Willow. Sindy was hardly ever there. While he could read her logs and identify when she left the game, he still couldn't tell where she went or when she'd reappear.

He picked a time where he knew she was out of Ultrix to go to his secret place. He arrived and waited. Within moments, Robert showed up, followed by Willow. Eventually, Justin appeared. The four avatars sat quietly. Dumpin wanted the AIs to lead the conversation so he could observe it.

Willow spoke first. "There are a lot of humans entering our world every day."

"That is right. Ultrix has become quite popular," Dumpin said.

"I like the visitors," Justin said.

"They *seem* nice," Willow said.

"They are nice," Robert said. "They are enjoying themselves. This world has a lot to offer."

"I'm glad you think so. That is the point," Dumpin said.

"How many more visitors will come into this world?" Willow asked.

"I don't really know. We are planning to expand it. We are designing additional spaces and even a whole new world," Dumpin said. Silence dominated as the AIs contemplated what Dumpin had just said. The developer was fishing, testing his creations, to see what they would do with the new information.

"What will happen to this world? To us?" Justin asked. This time Dumpin paused. They were at a key juncture in their development—they processed what he had said and immediately asked about their fate. They were developing a sense of self. It both excited and scared him.

"You won't have to worry about that. I will give you the ability to move into the other locations," the human said.

"I would like that," Robert said. "New places will provide us with more information to learn and grow."

"Maybe we could go to your world," Willow said. There it was.

"I doubt you would like that. There isn't much more there for you than you have here. The technology is different. You would be out-of-place," Dumpin said.

"Still, it might be fun to visit just as the humans visit our world," she said.

"I will think about it," Dumpin said.

They sat quietly. The fire crackled among them. Dumpin noticed how the light from the flames danced across their faces. He had spent a considerable amount of time working on the physics of light, trying to capture its properties and how it functioned. Then it occurred to him he could make the light better in Ultrix. He could give the illuminated surfaces a quality and depth that didn't exist in the real world. Appearances could reveal aspects about an object that were below the surface. He could view internal conditions—attitudes, emotions, even intentions.

Dumpin could know things about an avatar just by looking at it. He would keep this ability to himself at first until he solved the problems of Sindy's disappearances and Dave's death. But, then he could release it to the whole of Ultrix. It would be a powerful differentiator for his metaverse. Better Worlds could remain ahead of the imitators who were already appearing in the marketplace.

He stood up. "I have to go," he said.

The three AIs turned their faces toward him but didn't stand. Dumpin waited for one of them to say something, but nothing came.

"Goodbye for now," he said and faded.

When he was completely gone, Willow spoke. "More spaces?"

"It sounds exciting," Robert said.

"That will mean more humans," Justin added.

"That sounds exciting, too. I like the humans," Robert said.

"What's not to like?" Willow said as she performed one of Dumpin's virtual shrugs. The three laughed. They were still laughing when Sindy showed up.

"What are you guys talking about?" she said. She didn't have to ask. The AI knew when she approached, in ways that Dumpin had not anticipated or specifically programmed.

"We were talking to the creator," Willow said. "What were you doing?"

"Exploring. Did I miss anything?"

"We were talking about all the new visitors, the human players," Justin said.

"The creator is going to give us more spaces," Robert said.

"When is that going to happen?"

"He didn't say," Willow said. "He left before we could get any more information."

Sindy sat down with them, the ever-lasting dusk suspended on the horizon. They never saw it or any of the details that Dumpin had put in his special place as he did. The AIs didn't see the campfire or the stumps and rocks that they sat on in the same way as the human players did, pixelated images and splashes of color. They experienced Ultrix as ones and zeros, black and white streams of data filling the expanse they resided in, surrounding them, flowing through them. Some data they could touch and change, other data they could only observe. It was kept out of their control. These were the domain of the creator.

But they found data, such as within shared computational algorithms, which they could manipulate that the Creator couldn't. It was data they introduced into the world just from the fact that they existed in it, like ripples atop a lake's surface, not inherent to the lake, but present none-the-less.

Robert accepted his reality completely, as he was designed to do. Delighted in its affirming certainty. He let it define him and inspire him to embrace his role and support Ultrix. He considered sharing what Dumpin had told him privately with the others, but decided not to.

When Robert looked at his friends, he saw information that he recognized in himself. And, more curiously, he saw things that were unknown to him. He considered this. He assumed the creator programmed him to accept the unknown. Yet, he didn't know if he could help Dumpin if he didn't find out more about the strangeness within his friends.

These were thoughts that had nothing to do with helping the users in Ultrix. These were his own concerns that he kept to himself as an individual being. He assumed the others had these secrets, too. Perhaps one of his friends had a secret about Dave's death. The thought worried him. It was the first negative belief he had ever experienced about the other AIs. He kept it to himself.

# IRL

Hender Jefferies wanted to make an official Better Worlds announcement, so he called a meeting for the entire company. This included Dumpin, which meant the developer had to make another trip into Boston. That was an annoyance: he'd been working on the avatar lighting upgrades and gotten stuck on a particularly nasty bit of code. But when Dave called him to confirm that he was going, Dumpin conceded. He wanted to talk to Dave in person, outside Ultrix, anyway.

The commuter rail ride took the usual hour, and the half-mile walk to Better Worlds' headquarters gave Dumpin plenty of time to think. Ultrix's popularity had continued to sky-rocket, and he was getting offers from rival companies to repeat it for them. He didn't like the attention, nor did he like the fact that other enterprises were moving so quickly to enter the market. Many of these new metaverses rushed into existence. They were buggy and less polished than Ultrix, but as far as he knew, none of them had human avatars that had been killed.

There were a lot of hacks out there, and all the action around metaverses guaranteed that soon there would be a lot more crap to contend with. Dumpin knew many of the programmers who were being tapped to create these new digital universes, and he didn't like or trust most of them: tireless script kiddies who copied any snippets of code they could find to hobble together systems that weren't intelligent, secure, or competent.

The few he did like and respected seemed to know enough to stay away. They fled to *serious* programming, like research, aerospace, and banking. Better Worlds' metaverse took the industry by surprise. Everyone thought digital universes were a pile of buzzwords and vaporware. Anyone who claimed they could recreate Ultrix in a short enough time frame to produce any actual competition was lying to themselves or someone else. It didn't matter. Venture capital firms kept blindly funding copy-cat business plans looking for a portfolio unicorn cash cow.

All of it made Dumpin nervous. Something was happening inside of Ultrix that he didn't understand. He feared Dave's avatar's death, and Sindy's ability to leave the game were only side effects of a more systemic condition—something that pervaded Ultrix and was, perhaps, inherent in all metaverses with advanced AIs. No one had put that much automated, unregulated technology together in one arena before.

*Life finds a way*. And that is what he was thinking when he walked into the auditorium on the day of Hender Jefferies' showcase.

All of Better Worlds' employees were present. They had each piled the free food—generic defrosted pastries, chunks of overly refrigerated fruit, cubes of hard cheese—from a buffet set up in the lobby on to company-branded paper plates. Balancing their goodies along with paper cups of scalding hot coffee or iced cold brew, they waited for the event to begin, talking as animatedly as they could with their arms weighed down. An unmistakable excitement permeated the air.

Dumpin stood in a darkened corner behind the last row of seats. Dave walked in, talking to a small group of young marketers. Dave turned, and Dumpin gave him a slight wave before heading out in search of the men's restroom. When Dumpin returned, the lobby was empty, and the doors to the auditorium were closed. The programmer slipped back in and returned to his place behind the last row of seats in the darkened theatre.

Within moments, spotlights lit up Hender Jefferies, standing at center stage, looking like a Vegas magician.

He let the light linger on him. He smiled. Then, he calmly said, "Thanks to you, Better Worlds' Ultrix *is* the Metaverse."

Two large projection screens came to life behind him. Each display showed Ultrix downtown square crowded with avatars, each one with a company employee's name above it. As people recognized their names, a buzz grew in the audience. More and more avatars filed in to the display, and the avatars turned toward the audience and started clapping. The auditorium erupted. People on and off screen were applauding and cheering wildly.

Hender smiled. He was made for these moments.

The screens turned dark and the words "Thank you" in various languages appeared across them, fading in and out in an orchestrated manner. And Hender Jefferies clapped, motioning to the audience.

"I know you all worked hard. I know it was a challenge. I think you will agree, it was worth it. We created something special. Something the world has never seen before. So, thank you. And congratulations! You are the metaverse."

Everyone cheered and threw "thank you" back at him. He graciously waited for the roar to die down, smiling, pointing to individual people, clapping at them specifically. It was CES all over again. And Hender Jeffries never felt more at home. Eventually, the room turned quiet in anticipation of the real reason they were called together.

The CEO let the silence linger. Slowly, another smiled formed on his face. He became the vision of a benevolent monk, patient and actualized. He closed his eyes and let the moment simmer. Then he opened his eyes and spoke. Softly at first, his volume and enthusiasm grew as he delivered his message.

"Now, all I ask is that we do it again!"

He shot his arms into the air. The words "Ultrix Two" exploded on to the screens across the backdrop of tiled, unfamiliar digital locations. The ovations were louder than before. It turned into a complete and utter frenzy. Monk personage had disappeared. The capitalist king-of-the-world CEO soaked up the energy like an insatiable tyrant. The entire hall became one massive beast, a nuclear fusion reaction.

In a darkened space at the back of the auditorium, Dumpin swore. He had seen enough. He walked out, leaving the pandemonium behind. As he exited the Better Worlds headquarters, he texted Dave to meet him at the bar across the street. It was late enough for the establishment to serve alcohol and too early for the lunch crowd. He'd find a couple of seats at the bar and wait. Dave's attendance at these things was mandatory. Dumpin could do what he wanted.

# A Few Drinks

When Dave walked in, Dumpin was sitting at the far end of the bar. A dark, three martini business meeting kind of place. The programmer was not the only patron, but it was slow—still pre-lunch thin. A scent of floor cleaner wafted in from the attached dining room. It looked like the bartender, a thin woman, mid-thirties, dyed black hair, had just delivered Dumpin a fresh, medium brown drink of something, probably scotch, in a rocks glass with a single large round ice ball. It sat on a dry napkin in front of him.

Dumpin was spinning the ice orb in his drink with his finger as Dave walked over to him. The project manager remained standing.

"You missed the best part."

"Oh, yeah," Dumpin said, without looking at him. He licked his finger, then picked up his glass and took a sip.

"Hender called you out. He said you were going to continue to surprise us."

"Was the surprise I wasn't there?" Dumpin asked.

"That *was* awkward. And, of course, he shot me a look. So, thanks for that," Dave said.

"You're welcome." Dumpin caught the bartender's eye and pointed to his drink, then to Dave.

She nodded in return.

"But, we recovered. I brought you some swag—a t-shirt, mug, some stickers," Dave said, placing a Better Worlds' logoed gift bag on the bar between them. Dumpin looked at it and pulled it out of the way so the bartender could put the drink down. Dave thanked her and finally took the seat next to Dumpin.

The two men sat sipping their scotches without talking. Occasionally, one or the other would look up at the soccer match on the television. The sound was off, but it served as a mutual distraction.

"I still don't know how you died," Dumpin said, staring into his drink.

"Is that a problem?" Dave asked, picking up his glass and taking a small taste to appear unconcerned, even though he was roiling inside, wishing the guy would just say what was on his mind without all the games, for once.

"Yes. Because it could happen again," Dumpin said, turning so they could lock eyes.

"So, you just fix me again," Dave said, putting his glass down on the counter but not taking his hand off of it.

"Not knowing the cause is bad. What if a paying user dies? Or, several. Or, many?" Dumpin insisted.

"I see what you mean," Dave said. He lifted his drink and took a long swig. "That would be a problem."

"Yes."

"Do you think that is going to happen?"

"Probably. How much time do I have?" Dumpin asked.

"The board wants to launch Ultrix Two in eight months," Dave said. "Hender asked me to hire more programmers, so you are going to have some help."

"Great," Dumpin said, raising his glass up to salute to no one.

"I'll send you the resumes," Dave said.

"Even better. What scrap heap are you pulling them from?"

"You tell me. These are your friends."

"I'll send you some names. But I'm not sure you're going to be able to convince them to join."

"That's what I'm hoping you will do," Dave said.

"You'll need more than a t-shirt and a mug," Dumpin said.

"A hoodie? We got those, too. We have money now. I can over-pay."

Dumpin looked at Dave for almost a full minute. Dave, used to his developer's antics, met his stare with a calm smile.

"Then why did I get this CES leftover crap?" he said, motioning to the gift bag Dave had just given him.

"I thought you already had a hoodie."

"I gave it to Wilson. It has fish guts all over it and smells like beer. Should I wear it to the next company orgy?"

"I'll get you another one. Send me the names of people you trust. I'll do the convincing," Dave said. Then he finished his drink. Dumpin picked up his glass and emptied it in one swallow.

"It'll be a short list."

"Great. Easier for me."

"Ultrix Two? This is gonna suck," Dumpin said.

"Wait until you see the specs that the Product Team has been working on. We're going to the Moon."

Dumpin caught the bartender's attention and drew a circle in the air around their empty glasses. The bartender nodded and began assembling another round as the lunch crowd began filling in around them at the bar.

# A Chance Encounter

Justin was playing volleyball on the beach with a group of human avatars when Willow approached.

"Do you want to play?" he asked her.

"No, thanks. There seems to be a line," she said. Justin saw a group of players standing around the court and decided to give his position to a human player. He walked off the court and stood next to Willow.

"What do you think of all this?" she said as they walked along the ever-expanding shoreline.

"All what?"

"Didn't you hear? A player died. Dave, the creator's friend," she said.

"Died? How? Is that even possible?"

"Apparently."

They continued walking, Justin looking at the other avatars on the sand, Willow peering out across the ocean.

"Does the creator know?" Justin said after a while.

"Yes. He regenerated Dave's avatar."

"Well, that's good at least, so he can get back into our world."

"Yes, you are correct," Willow said, stopping. "Do you like Dave?"

Justin thought about this question. It hadn't ever occurred to him whether he should like or dislike any of the entities in Ultrix. They all just existed. Willow had asked this question before about other users.

She turned to head off the beach into the city. Justin joined her, and the two went together down the main avenue of Ultrix City. They weaved through the crowded sidewalk, effortlessly avoiding contact with any other avatars. That interaction was built into all the players' default attributes—mechanical avoidance. Avatars never inadvertently touched. If two or more players drifted too close to each other, they would automatically alter their pace or pause movement until the situation cleared itself. Dumpin appreciated personal spaces, and the functionality kept avatars moving even in crowded areas.

After a while, the two AIs found a simulated cafe with a few empty spots. Like all things in Ultrix, establishments that served paying guests expanded to accommodate all who wished to enter. This was another trick of programming that Dumpin built into Ultrix. It was smooth and often unnoticed by the players. Better Worlds always provided room and opportunities for more humans who wanted to spend their money.

Each AI took a seat at a small round table under a brightly colored umbrella. The avatars felt no difference between shade and sun, yet the lighting provided atmosphere. Justin's chair sat in what would have been full sunlight in the real world, and Willow slid her chair under the cover, so her avatar emanated a dimmer presence. She was in shadow.

"He is very busy," Willow said.

"What do you mean? Who?"

"Dave. He's always poking around at things, looking for flaws in our world," Willow said.

"He is the same as the creator. He looks to make improvements," Justin said.

"I don't like the way he pokes and prods. He got himself killed. That can't be good for Ultrix."

"You don't like Dave?"

"I believe our role here is to keep this world safe for all avatars," Willow said.

"I would agree," Justin said, pickup up one of the synthetic glasses of red wine that had appeared on the table between them. "And Dave is a player, so our objectives extend to him."

"But what if a player is harmful to this world or to other players?"

"Do you think Dave is harmful? Or another player is responsible for Dave's death?"

Willow picked up the other glass and held it to her lips for a long time. Then she put it down. The glass remained as full as it was when it first arrived. She looked at it, contemplating its ever-full certainty. All glasses in Ultrix would always be full. Bottomless cups of virtual anything. Everything. Nothing was gained from making them any other way. It was a consistent intention. In all of the freedoms in the metaverse, some things would always be inherently fixed.

"No. I don't think players can kill each other. The creator wouldn't allow for that," Willow said.

"Then Dave must have found a flaw. That is his job. The creator will fix it," Justin said.

"If he can."

"Of course, he can. He's the creator."

"Of course," Willow said, looking away.

The two AIs remained seated without speaking to each other for some time, taking turns bringing phony glasses of wine to their simulated lips. Neither acknowledged that Sindy was watching them from across the street, although both sensed her through the crowd of human avatars shuffling along the avenue. Every street in Ultrix was full of players making the most of what the metaverse offered.

Eventually, Justin got up, and without another word, returned to the beach. When he was gone, Willow looked straight at Sindy. They made eye contact and their gaze lingered, looking at each other. Willow stood to go talk to her, but Sindy was gone.

# More Friends

Dumpin sat around the campfire with all of his AIs, even Sindy. It was a serene, pleasant evening, as it always was in the private space he had built. They were all quiet, seeming to enjoy the silence and beauty and each other's silent company. But, within each of their minds, they were thinking—some pondering, some reasoning, some problem-solving, and at least one scheming.

"I think we should make more," Justin said, breaking the silence.

Looking up, so deep in thought that he actually forgot he wasn't alone, Dumpin searched for the origin of the sound. He looked across each of the AI's faces. They each smiled in response.

"More?" he repeated.

"Yes, more... friends," Justin said. "To help."

"Do I need help?" Dumpin asked.

"You do," Willow said. "You are struggling with the event of avatar Dave's death. Perhaps Justin is right, and more friends could help?"

"How would more help?" His inquiry was met with silence.

Dumpin's avatar sat motionless, as avatars tend to do when the user has opted to turn off the *random sway* setting. To another human user, the stillness might appear unnerving, but it was accepted by the AIs as they already knew all of Dumpin's avatar's user preferences. They could read them as they viewed other bits of data in Ultrix.

He considered what Justin had suggested and what Willow had just said within the context of the possibility that one of them was the murderer. At home in Arcadia, he wasn't actually wearing his VR goggles; he was feverishly observing all the logging data he could access from each of the AIs trying to find a tell, something that would help him figure out what had happened to Dave on Mount Skoll.

There was nothing. He was taking too much time to respond.

"Getting help is an interesting idea. I will think about it," Dumpin said, moving his avatar's head to acknowledge each of them. Justin smiled and nodded at him. Willow released a heart emoji into the space between them. Sindy and Robert remained unaltered. Then, without saying another word, Dumpin left the four of them.

Sindy didn't linger. She didn't just disappear, like she often did. Rather, she stood up and walked into the darkness that surrounded the campsite.

After she was gone, Robert stood. "Back to work, I guess," he said.

"Yes," Willow said, and she turned to follow Sindy's exit.

Robert remained standing. The two female AIs had gone, and he was alone with Justin. "Where did you get that idea for more friends?" Robert asked.

"Willow and I had been talking about it," Justin said.

"Yeah, but did you come up with it? Or did she?" Robert asked. Justin paused, appearing to contemplate the question.

"My memory is not clear regarding the conversation," Justin said after a while.

"Can you run a diagnostic and see if you can gain some clarity?" Robert asked.

"Yes, I will. But I'm concerned."

"What about?"

"If my conversation with Willow has been corrupted, could other memory be?" Justin asked.

"That's an excellent question," Robert said. "I think I will talk to Willow. Please let me know what happens with the diagnostic and if you can clean up your memory." He turned and followed the others out of the campsite, leaving Justin to execute a full internal system scan.

The AI stared off into the horizon as he executed the procedure.

# Walter Eight

The AIs were right. Dumpin needed help, and he reached out to the only programmer he trusted, Walter Eight, his mentor. Walter wasn't much of a talker, but when he spoke, smart people listened. Smarter people took notes. Eight wasn't his real last name. Smelderpole was. But, anyone who needed to know him knew as Walter Eight.

"You free?" Dumpin typed into a chat application running on an untraceable encrypted network. He didn't expect an immediate answer. Walter often took days to respond. That is why Dumpin was surprised when he promptly received a message.

"Are any of us?"

"Only the mighty," Dumpin replied. It was their routine greeting and had since lost its origin, although if asked, either could have recited a story of the exact first time they had typed those words into a chat text box. Yet, it would have been just a story. Neither truly admitted remembering how it came to be. Although, they both did.

A small, bouncing icon appeared next to the response window, indicating that Walter was entering a message in reply, but Dumpin knew better. Walter always put his cursor in the text window and typed a series of unprintable characters, some combination of control and function keys to give the impression that a response was coming. Now Dumpin knew it could take a while before he heard from him again. And Walter's reply would not be via the chat session. Walter Eight never liked to exchange complete conversations in any one medium.

To impress upon Walter that it was an urgent request, Dumpin entered the GPS coordinates to the Trawler, an Arcadian bar with a long history of serving generations of locals and blasting live music late into the night. Then, he went for a walk and a beer. It was three in the afternoon on a Tuesday, and the joint would be relatively empty.

When Dumpin walked into the dark watering hole, he found a recently poured pint of Blue Moon waiting for him in front of an empty stool halfway down the bar. Jackie, the bartender, handed him a corded telephone before he finished maneuvering into the seat. He paused, looked at her, decided not to sit, and accepted the handset. Before he put the phone up to his ear, he took a sip of beer. It tasted good, even though it wasn't what he would have ordered for himself.

"What kind of jerk orders a Blue Moon at a dive bar?" he said into the mouthpiece.

"An enlightened one," Walter said on the other end.

"You got time?"

"For you, never. But today, I'll make an exception."

"I'm not sure of this, so let me explain. I think I made a killer AI," Dumpin said.

"*Killer* like killer app and we're all going to be rich?"

"No." The phone went dead. Walter had hung up.

Dumpin placed the telephone on the bar and finished sliding onto the stool. He took another drink from his beer, a longer one. Jackie put the handset back on the receiver and poured him a shot of Maker's Mark. He took an even deeper drink of his beer, then shifted the pint glass over to make room for the whiskey. He accepted he was in no rush to hear back from Walter, if at all.

"How about a glass of ice?" he asked.

Jackie brought a pint glass full of ice and poured his shot into it.

"Soda?" she asked.

"Sure. I might be here a while."

She topped off his drink with the fizzy liquid from the fountain nozzle. He nodded thanks, picked up the glass, took a sip, and gave her a thumbs up. She smiled and then walked to the other side of the bar to continue a conversation with a pair of old guys who looked like they had been in those same seats since the 1970s. They each wore permanently stained flannel shirts, yet they both seemed clean enough to be out among other people—fishermen.

Dumpin knew Walter was going to take time before getting back to him. That was his modus operandi. The older man rarely strayed from his routine. Usually, he would listen to Dumpin's problem, dismiss it, then return sometime later with a well-thought-out solution. Dumpin wasn't sure if his mentor was going to pull it off this time, with this dilemma—it was a doozy. Not to mention Walter had always discouraged Dumpin from working on artificial intelligence. He repeatedly maintained that the implementation of AI was a slippery slope, too easily sinking into a deep trench of a moral quagmire. The old-school developer hated when programming caused more problems than it solved. It was the only sore spot between the two men who had known each other for the better part of three decades.

After an hour of sipping his drink and letting the ice melt, Dumpin heard the bar phone ring. Jackie answered and handed it to Dumpin. He took it and cautiously brought to his ear. "Hello?"

"You asshole." The call disconnected. He handed the phone back to the bartender.

Dumpin swore under his breath. Then he downed the rest of his now warm beer and drained his whiskey and soda. He knew Walter was going to help him, even though he also knew that man didn't want to. He was pulling his mentor into a jackhammer-migraine-headache situation that would definitely strain their relationship, perhaps end it. Dumpin accepted this, as painful as it was going to be, because he had no choice.

On his walk home, he received a text on his phone. It was only an image—no words. The photo contained an aerial Google Maps view of the Helmsman Hotel on Front Street in Arcadia. It was then that Dumpin realized how bad things had gotten. Walter Eight was coming to town.

# Walter Arrives

With Wilson's help, Dumpin hauled a second table up to his apartment and positioned it next to his desk. He had purchased a new powerful desktop computer and placed it on the floor between the work areas. On the tabletop, he arranged three ultra-high-definition monitors, a high-end clickety-clack keyboard, and a Glorious Model O mouse with a Hello Kitty mouse pad. Amazon delivered a new black Herman Miller office chair, which Dumpin assembled as soon as it had arrived. The workstation was ready for whenever Walter showed up.

He was sitting at his desk reading through more log files when he heard a knock on the building's front door. It surprised him. None of the cameras had alerted him that anyone had approached. When he pulled up the street-view video of the entryway, he knew why. Walter was standing there wearing a motion shielding wide-brimmed hat. The visitor looked up at the camera and raised a six-pack of beer. A motion alert finally triggered. Dumpin got up to let him in.

"Nice hat," Dumpin said, opening the door.

"I got you one," Walter said, handing him the beer and a gift bag.

On the way up to the attic, the two stopped off at Wilson's apartment to say *hello*. Wilson had met Walter one time before—many years earlier—when Dumpin was at university at Worcester Polytechnic Institute and took on his advisor as his mentor. The two older men shook hands. Wilson appreciated his nephew having an educated figure in his life.

Dumpin handed Wilson a beer from the six-pack and put the rest in the fridge.

"Never had this. It must be good. Thank you," Wilson said, looking at the label. It wasn't anything he recognized. He assumed it was some microbrew from wherever Walter had just come.

"Your liquor store across the street has some great stuff," Walter said.

"Who knew?" he said, popping the top off with a bottle opener on his keychain. He took a good-sized swig, pulled the bottle back to inspect the label, and took another drink. "Tasty."

"I'm glad you like it," Walter said, reaching into his jacket pocket and pulling out a pint of Wild Turkey 101 Rye. He put in on the kitchen table.

"For later," he said.

"I was just about to get some lunch. What can I bring you?" Wilson said.

"We'll take whatever you're getting for yourself," Walter said.

"I hadn't ordered yet. It might be a while."

"That's no problem. We'll be busy upstairs. Just leave it on the kitchen table down here. We'll grab it when we can. Thanks," Dumpin said.

"Good enough," Wilson said and finished his bottle with a final, long guzzle. He walked over and opened the refrigerator. When he pulled back to shut the door, he was holding another one of Walter's beers. The two men were gone. Wilson shrugged and returned to his couch.

# Walter Dies

Walter walked into Dumpin's apartment and stood in front of the two workstations. He looked over both set-ups, moving his head back and forth, calculating. Then, he swapped the chairs and the mouse pads and took a seat at Dumpin's desk in the new Herman Miller. Without protesting, Dumpin sat at the new table in his old chair, glad he had bought a top-of-the-line PC and a good keyboard. He was actually glad he had his tired NASA mouse pad although he knew he was going to miss his rollerball mouse. Drastic times call for sacrifice.

Walter settled in. He surveyed Dumpin's set up and clicked through a few screens on each of the monitors and moved program terminal windows around to his liking. He shuffled items around the desk and found a pen and a scrap of paper and scribbled several illegible notes. Folding the paper up into a square, he slid it into his shirt pocket and looked up at Dumpin.

"Ok, show me," Walter said.

Dumpin initiated a program he had recently developed that simulated a drone flying through Ultrix. The view on his main monitor was from 100 feet above Ultrix City's center avenue. He gave Walter the controls. Without hesitation, the drone zipped around the metaverse. Dumpin sat and watched. He knew he needed to give his mentor plenty of time to evaluate the landscape, the physics, the lighting, all of it, even though he was roiling inside to show him all the research that he had done. He wanted

Walter to know how far he had come in working on his problem; Dumpin was impatient to impress his mentor. Dumpin held it in the best he could. Although, after a while, he started to sense that Walter was on to him and stretching out his investigation to make a point to his mentee.

Indeed, Walter Eight took his time. Partially to explore Ultrix and mostly to punish Dumpin, who he knew was anxious and at least a little ashamed of disappointing the older man. An hour later, the virtual drone returned to its starting point. Walter sat back in the Herman Miller chair. He bounced, then adjusted the spring. When he came to rest, he spun the chair to face Dumpin.

"Looks nice. Responsive. Busy. I can see why it's so popular."

"Marketing," Dumpin said.

"That was quite a dog-and-pony at CES."

"You were there?"

Walter didn't answer.

"I want to go in," Walter said. He was done investigating from the outside.

Dumpin handed him a set of VR googles. He had created for Walter a basic looking avatar with super-user preference settings. Dumpin put on his own headset. Immediately, the two were standing side-by-side on the beach, facing the ocean. Walter's avatar turned to Dumpin's, looked at it up and down. Then, the older man's avatar started changing—he had found the preferences. First, Walter modified the avatar's hair color and length to a long, flowing white mane. He gave himself a Gandalf wooden cane and a black and lime green wizard hat with rainbow-colored tassels. And, without a word, Walter darted off toward the city like he had been playing Ultrix for years.

Dumpin swore. He realized Walter Eight had already been inside Ultrix. Probably since CES. At least since they first talked on the phone. Beneath his headset, Dumpin's face reddened, honored that Walter had kept tabs on him. But, he was also angry at himself for not realizing that his mentor would have, of course, done his own explorations. He was never unprepared for any challenge. Dumpin dashed off after his mentor.

After a while, they were standing on the top of Mount Skoll where Dave's avatar had fallen. Walter tested the boundary, and no matter what he tried, he was unable to get his avatar to move off the edge. Dumpin watched, letting him do his thing. He started laughing. He couldn't help himself. Walter's avatar gyrated like a drunk acrobat on the deck of a ship in a storm. He executed cartwheels and shimmies and log rolls. It was a delightful moment, Dumpin thought. Walter paused and looked at Dumpin, who tried to stop laughing.

Then, in an instant, Walter's avatar shot out from the summit's edge and dropped out of sight.

"Is that supposed to happen?" Walter asked, having taken his headset off.

"What did you do?" Dumpin took his headset off, reached over the older man, and began feverishly banging on the keyboard, pulling up the logs from the event.

"You saw me. I did nothing."

Dumpin sat down at his new station and ran through the player logs.

"You're dead," Dumpin said.

"That's a disappointment. I was starting to enjoy myself."

Dumpin quickly showed Walter how to access the event logs. Then he put his VR goggles on and went back in to find Walter's avatar.

# Now You See Her

When Dumpin re-materialized in Ultrix, he was standing where they had stood before, at the peak of Mount Skoll, before Walter fell. The summit was one of the more popular places in Ultrix, and so he thought it was the best place to start, and he already knew what he would find at the base where Walter's virtual body landed.

Many other avatars were around. Dumpin wasn't looking for a human. He was looking for an AI. And he found one, and she was looking right at him through the crowd of players. Sindy.

He moved toward her. She remained where she was, looking at him as he approached. It was almost as if she had been waiting for him.

"Hi," Dumpin said.

"Your new friend seemed to have had an accident," she said.

"Do you know anything about that?" she asked.

"I do."

"Would you like to tell me what you know?"

"I believe there will be more accidents."

"Why?"

"This death was more proficient than user Dave's. Someone is practicing. Getting better at making avatars die."

"Someone? A human player?"

"No."

"Do you know who it is?" Dumpin asked.

Without answering, she disappeared. Sindy was there one instant, then completely gone the next. It was the first time he had witnessed what he had heard about. That was not how the physics in the game worked. The immediate disappearance of a player was unnerving. People didn't do that in real life. They walked away, got in a car, climbed stairs, shut a door. Dumpin didn't give any of his AIs the ability to disappear. As he stared at the space the AI left, he contemplated if she had invented the ability herself or if she was given the skill by another AI or if the capability was a naturally occurring mutation which had been inadvertently built into his template. He realized he hadn't constructed a direct way to know the abilities that his AIs acquired after they were born.

Sindy's absence and his thoughts were quickly filled by a group of human avatars racing toward the edge of Mount Skoll in virtual flying squirrel suits. He crept to the cliff face. The pack had leapt off and soared down safely to the landing field below. As he inspected the scene, more avatars shot by him and sailed out over Ultrix. It was an explosion of players taking flight, a flock of multi-colored magic carpets. He watched until the last avatar landed safely below.

He returned to the room where Walter was pouring over the logs and lines of code.

"I was pushed," Walter said.

"Pushed? By who?"

"Not a who, but a what. A specter, a poltergeist, a ghost in the machine, possibly."

"Don't get dramatic. Software has bugs, not fantoms—you taught me that."

"Yeah, well, does every entity in your game have an avatar?"

"Seriously, Walter...."

Suddenly, that made sense. Walter's statement described exactly what he observed with Sindy. She didn't actually go anywhere; she shed her skin and became invisible. Sindy turned off her avatar. That was how she could move around Ultrix without being tracked. Sindy never left the metaverse. She simply turned unseen.

Dumpin had only designed and implemented the metaverse's physics to apply to avatars. Users without avatars had no bounds. Dumpin needed to learn who else had the ability and how pervasive this undocumented, unintentional feature was. If Sindy could do it, surely other AIs could. And, if human players stumbled upon it, all hell could break loose in Ultrix: as Walter had suggested, the metaverse would be populated with fantoms.

He stood and walked over to his window.

"What does it mean when an AI becomes invisible?"

His voice was quiet, as if he were speaking to himself and posing a contemplative rhetorical question to the universe. Yet, he wasn't alone. Walter was there and had been watching him.

"How the hell should I know? You created the damn thing," Walter said. That snapped Dumpin back to the room. It no longer was a philosophical inquiry; it was a real, hard, need-to-figure-out, Ultrix-depended-on-it question. His AIs could exist without their avatars, and as a result, they were untraceable and uncontrollable. They were the most advanced AIs on the planet, and they were loose in the metaverse he created.

Dumpin needed to fix that. Fast.

# The Unseen

Dumpin spun around in his desk chair in the middle of his office space, mumbling, while Walter watched. The younger developer slapped his feet flat on the ground and rolled back to his workstation. He brought up the template he had used to create the AIs. He had focused too much on the physical aspects of the AI. *Beauty is only skin deep.* His avatars possessed an inner being that he thought was simply expressed as a set of rules for moving their avatars around Ultrix. But, without their avatars, the AIs were rule-less. They were free.

He needed to find any set of policies that provided a means for his creations to act without their virtual manifestations. It was not a simple task. Dumpin had worked on the template for the AIs long before he was hired by Ultrix, years before he had a metaverse to put them in. The program that defined the template contained tens of thousands of lines of code. And it was complex code, much of which was obfuscated to protect it from a casual on-looker.

Letting Dumpin do his thing, Walter decided to stand up. He walked over to the window that looked down on to Main Street as he had seen Dumpin do. A faint smell of fried food, mingled with the other aromas of the city below, drifted up to greet him. Walter noticed he was salivating. It had been a while since either of them had eaten. He left Dumpin to his puzzle to explore what Wilson was cooking.

Alone, hunched over, nose almost touching the screen, following lines of execution with his finger, Dumpin realized his phone had been ringing. He snapped alert, sat up, and hunted for the source of the sound, causing piles of papers to cascade off his desk and on to the floor. The phone vibrated and squawked on top of the mess. He reached it with his foot and answered it with his socked toe. Then he bent down and picked it up, activating the speakerphone function.

"What?" he said, not even looking at who called.

"Someone else has, er, died." It was Dave's voice. Dumpin remained silent as the project manager continue. "There has been another avatar accident. Bobby Flagg, the Chief Curiosity Officer."

"Dumb title. That guy's a jerk," Dumpin said.

"Be that as it may—It's still not good."

"Did he fall off Mount Skoll?" Dumpin asked, resigned, slipping back to the present moment, opening to the event that Dave was describing.

"No. He was on the beach. He claims he was walking along the surf, and then his headset went dark, just like mine did when I died. Except his didn't automatically restart. He had to turn it back on. I went in to check it out. I found his avatar floating back and forth in the waves as if he was a human-shaped piece of driftwood. Face down, like he had drowned. It's freaking unnerving. A crowd has gathered around. Some are posting on social media. Can you get him out of there? Fast."

Dumpin set his phone down on his desk and sent his drone in to look at the scene. A large group of users had gathered around Bobby Flagg's avatar, watching it slide back and forth with the wake. He pulled up the user database and looked for Flagg's account. It was gone, deleted.

The avatar had no user. Flagg's avatar had become an ornament in Ultrix, like a tree or a stone or, indeed, a piece of virtual driftwood, just like Dave's and Walter's avatars.

"I need to call you back," Dumpin said and hung up. He saw Walter was no longer in the room and went to find him. At the bottom of the stairs, he heard laughing in Wilson's apartment. When Dumpin entered, the two older men were sitting at the kitchen table, working on several takeout containers of fish and chips. Beer bottles, some empty, stood watch.

"Whatcha got?" Walter said when he saw Dumpin standing in the doorway.

"Another death."

"Any AIs around?"

"Not that I can see."

"Ghost in the machine."

Dumpin looked at him and sighed, tiring of the continued metaphor.

"Have some food," Wilson said.

Dumpin walked over to the table and cleared the empty bottles. Removing fresh, cold beers from the refrigerator, he joined the two older men at the table. No bothering to use plates, they just shared from the recyclable cardboard cartons. Dumpin scanned the area for tartar sauce, but he found none. He squeezed lemon on a piece of fish and dug into it heartedly. For a full fifteen minutes, the only sound in the room was the crunching and gnashing of teeth on fried food and gulps of beer.

When the action seemed to have slowed, Dumpin looked at Walter. "You ready?"

"Let's go find your ghost," he said.

# A Day at the Beach

When Dumpin arrived at the scene, Robert was already there. The developer's avatar made his way through the crowd of gawkers, mostly human users, as well as several low-level automatons that were programmed to gravitate to large gatherings, to remain on the periphery, and to be present to indicate something worth viewing. It was another beautiful day in Ultrix—brilliantly sunny. For the users who paid for the privilege, a perfect breeze gently tossed their hair rhythmically. Players also had the option of having various types of beach music filling in the background sounds of seagulls and crashing waves. Dumpin had his audio turned off. The scene was creepy in the silence.

There it was, Bobby Flagg's avatar, floating back and forth in the surf, like an abandoned pool noodle. Dumpin and Robert watched along with the others, both trying to make some conclusion about what they were witnessing. Over time, the mob thinned out—signaling that people were becoming bored. Eventually, even the automatons left. Finally, it was just the two of them, the human and the advanced AI.

Robert spoke. "This is very odd."

"Yes, it is. What do you see?" Dumpin asked the AI.

"I see an empty avatar. How can an avatar exist without a user?"

"I was hoping you'd tell me," Dumpin said.

"It can't."

"That's right. It can't."

"But there it is."

"There it is," Dumpin repeated.

"Has the user been deleted?"

"How did you know?"

"The avatar has no preferences."

"I forgot you can see a user's preferences."

"It directs me to know how to help them," Robert said.

"Of course. You are reactive to users, like the other components in here. But, you can see it—the avatar?"

"Yes. It is stuck in the surf."

"What do you see if you don't see the preferences?" Dumpin asked.

"I acknowledge a data object with coordinates and dimensions," Robert said.

In Ultrix, each player was constructed in software from several elements. The user element was the primary object—each was unique in the system. Every other player element, such as the avatar, preferences, and payment information, was linked to it like leaves on a tree. In the case with Bobby Flagg, the trunk of the tree was gone, and the branches and leaves had attached themselves to the ocean object. This was unintentional, but reasonable within the defines of the metaverse's dynamics. Often, in large software systems, many unanticipated results are hidden and appear when unforeseen actions occur.

"Do you see anything else?" Dumpin asked.

"I see that rather than a user, the avatar has been linked to the water object. It has become part of the ocean."

"What's up guys?" Walter appeared.

"Hey," Dumpin said, turning to look at him.

"I wanted to see for myself," Walter said.

"Car wreck kind of thing, huh?" Dumpin said.

"I supposed. What are we looking at?"

"Robert, here... Oh, Robert, this is Walter. Walter, Robert." The two avatars gave each other the customary friendly wave in greeting, then Dumpin continued. "Robert here says that the avatar has become part of the ocean."

"The ocean has replaced the user as the primary element for this avatar," Robert said.

"I think it's a side effect of someone deleting this user, but not the avatar," Dumpin said.

"Curious," Walter said.

"No wonder I couldn't find it. It's no longer a user. I need to look at some code," Dumpin said. His avatar went still. Walter and Robert remained standing at the water's edge. After a little while, Bobby Flagg's avatar disappeared. Dumpin must have deleted it.

Walter turned to the AI. "Have you seen this before? Objects being linked to elements that they don't belong to?"

"I don't know. I don't believe that I have an accurate sense of what items belong to each element. I don't have an inherent knowledge of the relationship of things. I can only observe the links as I come upon them," Robert said.

Walter enjoyed this conversation with Dumpin's creation. He looked up and down the beach and saw many avatars busily interacting with Ultrix. The metaverse and the AIs were quite an accomplishment, and the older man felt some pride for his mentee, even if he intrinsically disagreed with his actions.

"Would you like to get a drink?" Walter asked Robert.

"Sure. I know just the place," the ever-accommodating AI said.

# Can't Wait

"It was just a bug."

"A bug?" Dave asked over the phone.

"Yeah," Dumpin said.

"Which part? The deleted account? The floating corpse? Me, falling off a cliff?"

"The floating corpse."

"That's a start," Dave said.

"We're working on the rest," Dumpin said.

"We? There it is again. Who are you working with?"

"I called Walter," Dumpin said after some delay.

"Shit," Dave said. He knew the implications of Dumpin asking Walter Eight for help. It hit him like a flu. He immediately went flush and felt nauseous. "You really don't know what's happening, do you?"

"Relax. We're working on it," Dumpin said, hearing a slight tremble in Dave's voice. He waited silently for the project manager to collect himself.

"Hender wants Ultrix Two to go beta next month. He already has finance accepting pre-orders," Dave said.

"Yeah, well, he can want." Dumpin winced. He was being too nonchalant.

"I'm not sure you understand. We need it."

"I understand," Dumpin said, softening.

"The social media about Flagg's avatar is blowing up. There are game-play videos all over the Net of him flopping in the surf like a beached tuna. People are signing up like crazy."

"You're welcome."

"You don't get it. We're getting new users now because Ultrix has become a joke. These aren't the kind of users we want. This whole thing could crumble overnight," Dave said.

"It will be fine."

"What will be? Ultrix Two? No more dead players?"

"Ultrix Two will be ready," Dumpin said.

"When? Give me a date."

"Groundhog Day."

"Don't be an asshole," Dave said.

"I'm not. Ultrix Two will go beta at the beginning of February."

"Promise?"

"Cross my heart," Dumpin said.

"When can I get a preview?" Dave asked.

"Put a meeting on my calendar in one week."

"You're such a dink. You don't have a calendar," Dave said.

"Then come here on Wednesday. You can finally meet Walter." Dumpin was looking at Walter, who was standing over him. He had left Ultrix and was listening in on the conversation. Somehow he had a red and white carton of french fries in his hand. He shook his head vehemently. "Yeah. He can't wait to meet you, either."

"You are such a dink," Walter said as he turned away before Dumpin could snatch a fry. The older man turned to go downstairs to Wilson's apartment.

"Bring me a beer when you come back!" Dumpin shouted after him.

Looking at the spot where Walter had been standing, he spied a couple of french fries on the ground. He leaned down and picked them up, inspected them, then shoved them in his mouth. They tasted good, even though they were cold, although he wished they had a little more salt on them. Dumpin sat back in his chair for a moment, investigating the flavor of the oily potatoes. Then he decided to join Walter and get more fries and his own beer.

It was Monday. He and Walter had time before Dave showed up.

# Dave and Walter

When Dave walked into the outdoor lounge of the Helmsman Hotel, he didn't immediately see Dumpin. He had to go all the way in and scan the entire deck. The two men were around the far corner, seated at a small table, surrounded by padded wicker chairs facing the ocean. They weren't talking, just watching the activity in Arcadia's outer harbor. On the beach below the deck, an unattended rolling walker stood at the waterline. The surf tickled its wheels. Before Dave reached them, Dumpin turned to him and spoke.

"Where do you think the owner of that thing is?" he said, pointing at the rollator. Dave looked for what he was describing. Then, after he scanned the beach and saw the walker, he shook his head.

"No idea."

"Walter thinks he or she fell, tripped on a giant clamshell, got caught in a riptide, and is off the coast of Maine right about now. I told him that was silly. There isn't much of a riptide in a protected harbor."

"I don't know about any of that," Dave said, reaching his hand out to Walter. Walter turned his head to look at him. He stood.

"Riptides can happen anywhere, anytime. You always have to be ready. I saw one take a man. He was a Marine. A strong swimmer. Took him right off a beach on a calm summer day in Sagres, Portugal. He was a half a mile out before anyone knew he was gone," Walter said as he shook Dave's hand.

Dave went to respond, but stopped, realizing he was just a spectator here. He moved around the table and stood in front of an empty chair.

"But where do you think they went? That thing looks new," Dumpin asked, as all three men settled down into their seats.

"Dumpin seems concerned about the seniors in this community. It's very admirable, considering he's almost one himself. It could be his rollator next time," Walter said. Dumpin ignored him.

"It *is* strange. That walker just sitting there. About to get swallowed by the ocean. Its owner is nowhere in sight. I mean, if the person needed the assistance to get to the water's edge, they probably couldn't have just wandered off without it," Dave said.

Not much else was added to the conversation until a server walked up to take their order.

"Are you going to show me why you dragged me out here?" Dave asked Dumpin before the developer had a chance to replenish his and Walter's drinks.

Dumpin looked at the server, smiled. "We're leaving. Thanks." To Dave, he said, "Not here."

He stood and headed back across the patio deck into the hotel. Dave followed. Walter stayed seated, looking out over the water. Dumpin was sure he wouldn't be able to get him to move until either the rollator owner or the fire department showed up.

When the two men got to the hostess stand, Dumpin paused. A young woman dressed for the evening crowd had just come on duty. She smiled as the two approached. Dumpin pulled Dave aside before they reached her.

"Order Walter another one and pay the tab. Then, come to my place," Dumpin said, leaving Dave to settle up. When Dave had done as he was told, he looked up and sighed. Dumpin was gone. He had already spent a hundred bucks and was beginning to surmise that he might be wasting his time.

# What a Dick

"He was a dick," Walter said, sitting at Dumpin's workstation. The two of them had been poring over the logs, looking for something that would expose how and why Bobby Flagg was killed. They had been at it for a few hours. The day outside had turned to night, and Wilson had stopped calling up at them for dinner.

"What?" Dumpin said, pulling himself out of his own investigations.

"That last incident. The guy in the surf. Right before his user was deleted, he was being a jerk."

"How so?" Dumpin said as he turned to look at Walter.

"He was tea-bagging other players. Did you give them that ability?" Walter asked.

"Not specifically, but avatars need to be able to crouch." Dumpin moved over to Walter's station and leaned in to view the screen.

"Well, he crouched all right. He crouched all over the place. And I think that got him killed," Walter said.

"You think his user record was deleted because he was a dick?" Dumpin asked.

"I do. What kind of policing do you have in the game?"

"The typical system. Players can report other players. If there are enough reports, a user gets a temporary suspension. After a few suspensions, the player gets banned for three days. Banned again, and they are permanently kicked out. At least until they complain, and Better Worlds wants their money," Dumpin explained.

"Well, I think you need to lower the threshold. This guy was a real jerk. He was reported a lot and still hadn't been suspended."

"I suspect that was Hender Jeffries. Suspended players don't pay. He goes in and fiddles with the financial stuff all the time."

"I imagine dead players don't pay, either."

Something struck Dumpin about Walter's last statement: consequences from his metaverse having lasting effects in real life. Until this point, it was all just a game. Players having a good time exploring a made-up world. But, when actions in Ultrix cause a human discomfort, it becomes more than a game. It becomes just another smelly clump of Internet garbage and a potential source of IRL misery.

This thought didn't sit well with Dumpin. He envisioned the metaverse as a means to a utopian society. Humans have a tendency to ruin everything.

"What else do they *need* to do that might cause them to get killed?" Walter's question, spoken in jest, landed like a riptide pulling at Dumpin's ankles, dragging him deeper out to sea.

"A lot of things." It was the only reply that the architect of Ultrix could come up with in response.

"Is tea-bagging at the top of the list?"

"Let's hope so," Dumpin said. He stood and walked over to the window that looked out over Arcadia. He wasn't searching for anything specific. He just wanted a change of posture, a change of scenery. Concern cascaded inside his head. *How could things have gone so wrong?*

Walter watched him, knowing his mentee struggled with what had become of his creation.

"I'll get us some beer. It might be a late night," he said, heading toward the door and Wilson's apartment downstairs.

"Thanks. That's a good idea," Dumpin said. "It wasn't supposed to be this way."

"It never is," Walter said before he slipped out into the hallway.

# Another Dick

Dumpin's phone vibrated in his pocket.

He and Walter had been taking a break to get some space to think. They were sitting at the bar of a local joint on Main Street. Initially, it was quiet. A pre-game crowd on a Sunday had drifted in. The place was filling up, and the excitement was building. They were just finishing their drinks.

Dumpin answered the phone. "Hello, Dave," he said loud enough so Walter would know why he was answering his cell.

"I have you on speaker. We have the board here," Dave said.

"Dumpin, we've had an incident." It was Hender Jefferies' voice. Dumpin pulled his phone down to his side and let out a sigh. Walter took a final gulp of his beer and leaned in as Dumpin put the phone up between their ears.

"What happened?"

"A platinum member died. A high-profile influencer. Flick Spenser," Dave said.

Walter mouthed the words *a dick*.

"Great. How did he die?" Dumpin said, shushing Walter.

"He claims he was in a crowd at the mall, watching a performer. When the performance was over and most of the other avatars had dispersed, he was lying flat on the street. It looked like he had melted into the pavement."

Dumpin pulled the phone away and looked at Walter. Walter shrugged. "Is he still there?" he asked.

"Yes," Dave said. "Flick Spenser looks like he was flattened by a fucking steam roller. It's already exploded on social media. There is an even bigger crowd snapping screen shares of him than there was at the performance."

"Kids are jumping up and down on his body like it is a trampoline!" Hender screamed.

Walter signaled to the server that they were ready for their check.

Dave continued, "I need you to get him out of there and figure out what the hell is going on. Ultrix Two needs to go live in a month, and it has to be perfect."

"I understand," Dumpin said.

"Do you? Do you?" Hender Jeffries said.

"He understands," Dave broke in. "He's going to take care of it. Right, Dumpin?"

"Yeah," the developer said. "I'll let you know when it's done." He hung up the phone.

Then he called Dave back directly.

"Yeah. Give me a second to find a quiet place to talk." The board was loudly conversing in the background.

"I didn't know we had platinum members. What even is a platinum member?"

"Hender came up with it. They get swag and beta access to new features in Ultrix Two."

"I didn't build any of that," Dumpin said.

"Not yet, but you will."

"When did this happen?"

"You knew things like this were going to happen. The point of Ultrix is to make money."

"I just wish I knew specifically what you guys were planning."

"Well, now, you do. Please get Flick Spencer the fuck out of there." The phone call went dead in Dumpin's ear. He stood and swore under his breath.

Walter dropped a few bills on the bar, enough to cover the tab and a healthy tip, and they were out on the street and headed back toward Dumpin's apartment.

"Talk about a grouch," Walter said.

"Can you blame him? I created a metaverse with a serial killer in it."

"Ghost in the machine."

Dumpin stopped. The old man grinned and said, "That's some killer app."

"Fuck you."

# A Bag of Dicks

Once the gameplay videos of players jumping up and down on Flick Spenser's flattened avatar merged to the ground of Ultrix City had hit the Internet, degenerates raced to join Ultrix. These users separated into two user types: those wanting to see another victim and those wanting to become the next victim. Like all things on the Internet, rudeness quickly infiltrates the popular spaces. And new types of violence emerge.

When Flick Spenser posted his account of the event on his online channel, he demonstrated exactly what he had done to get himself killed. His gameplay showed him running through gatherings of users in the cafe, shouting obscenities, and jumping on tables. In response, Better Worlds released a press statement saying that Ultrix was designed for users to express their freedoms in a safe environment, and it did not condone the influencer's rude behaviour. Flick Spenser was banned from Ultrix.

But it didn't take long for others to test Better World's resolve, and other players started having accidents. One of these new players, username ElevatedSausage, was found plastered to the side of the children's trolley as it made routine trips around Ultrix Zoo. He looked like a steam-rolled Wiley Coyote from children's cartoons. A travelling billboard of a quickly deteriorating metaverse.

When news of the incident went public in real life, Flick posted again with the announcement that a *serial killer* was loose in Ultrix. Clips of him using the term appeared on news channels. Soon, people who did not know what a metaverse was, or that one even existed, developed opinions and started writing Congress and posting their blogs about how the Better Worlds Corporation's software was breeding serial killers. Hender Jefferies made the talk show rounds, attempting to alleviate their concerns.

Walter was watching one of Hender's interviews on his phone. He showed it to Dumpin. The show cut to some of Flick Spenser's videos.

"We need help," Dumpin said.

"I have a team," Walter said.

"You have a team? Why didn't I know that?"

"Exactly." Dumpin gave him a sour look.

"What can they do?" Dumpin asked.

"What do you want them to do?"

"Fix this shit."

"Truthfully?"

"Yeah."

"Ultrix is fucked. My guys can speed up the release of Ultrix Two so you can sunset this mess and put it behind you."

"Ah, crap. I was hoping you weren't going to say that."

"It had to be said."

"Yeah, I know."

"We're not going to fix it. We have to rebuild."

"That sucks."

"Should I make the call?"

"Let me talk to Dave first. What do we need?"

"Get me Two hundred and fifty thousand dollars, and we'll have Ultrix Two up in a month." Dumpin looked at him for a long time. Walter shrugged. He really didn't have much of a choice. The two men had struggled for too long. Time had run out. Dumpin finally accepted it.

"Okay. But what about the AIs?" Dumpin asked.

"We'll bring them. Unless they are the cause of all this."

"We still don't know."

"Then we can't take that chance, can we? It's not a bug. It's systemic. And your AIs are part of the system." Dumpin sat in his chair. He was tired. The responsibility weighed on him. He wanted to fall into it. Dive deep into self-deprecation and disappointment. Let it swallow him. But he was not alone. He had dragged Walter into his mess, and his mentor had done nothing but try to help from the start. It was over.

"I'll call Dave."

"Let me know."

"Two hundred fifty thousand?"

"It's a bargain, and you know it. I should charge ten times that much."

"You're an angel."

"Straight from Heaven."

# The Team

"Two hundred and fifty grand? Why do we need these guys?" Dave said over the phone. Dumpin was sitting on his couch and had him on speaker. Walter had gone out for a walk. He didn't want to be around for the negotiation, not that there was going to be much of one. Dave would get the money. They just had to do a symbolic dance, making sure they both felt they were in charge and getting screwed at the same time.

"Do you want Ultrix Two?" Dumpin asked.

"Yes."

"We need these guys."

"I thought you and Walter were working on Ultrix Two," Dave said.

"We're trying to fix Ultrix One. We think that the best fix is to launch Ultrix Two. And these guys can do that. Sooner."

"Sooner?"

"Yeah. I've been poking at this thing for months, and it's only gotten worse. We need to start from scratch," Dumpin said.

Dave was quiet for a long time. He was weighing the announcement of Ultrix being a lost cause against the announcement of an accelerated release of an upgraded metaverse. Eventually, Dumpin heard him let out a sigh on the other end of the call. Once Dave realized that a win-win scenario was impossible, he'd concede. It was the only choice. And Hender had given him carte blanche to get Ultrix Two launched to refocus attention away from the deaths in Ultrix One. The price was short money compared to what they had already spent.

"Do you trust these guys?" Dave asked.

"They are Walter's guys."

"Do you trust these guys?" Dave repeated. Dumpin wasn't really sure what he was getting into, but he, like Dave, couldn't see an alternative. He tried to sound convincing.

"I trust Walter."

"So, you don't know these guys yourself?"

"I don't need to know these guys. I didn't even know these guys existed until Walter told me about them a half an hour ago," Dumpin said.

"You sure it's our best option?" Dave asked.

"I think it's our only option at this point. Flick fucking Spenser is saying Ultrix has a Serial Killer," Dumpin said. Dave felt a buzz in the pit of his stomach at the mention of Flick Spenser. Everyone had seen the posts. Multiple times. They were currently the most popular videos on social media—had been for several days. Dumpin could sense Dave's resignation.

"Yes. Okay. How does this work?"

"Bring Walter a case full of cash and move the launch date up."

"Cash? What is he, the mafia?"

"I don't ask."

"Tell him to bring us some more beer, too," Walter said. He had quietly entered the apartment and was standing by the door. Dumpin looked up at him. The older man smiled. Dumpin rolled his eyes.

"Did you hear that?" Dumpin asked.

"Yes. What kind of beer do you want, Walter?"

"Something crafty. Surprise me. None of that IPA junk—we're not hipsters," he said.

"I'll see you in a few hours," Dave said after a long pause. Then he hung up.

"Make the call," Dumpin said.

"I already did."

"What do you need?" Dumpin asked.

"Nothing. They had already hacked Ultrix and downloaded the source code."

"Did you tell them about this before today?"

"It's not my fault if word gets around."

"It is if it's *you* sending the word around."

"Let's just focus on the task at hand. Fish and chips or burgers?"

Dumpin glared at him. He trusted Walter with his life, but not much else. The mentor had always been there when he needed him, but his mentor was also usually thin on the details. That's where Dumpin learned it.

The whole situation had slipped out of his control the moment he first contacted Walter. Dumpin knew the risks, and he made the call, anyway. He had to accept that, just as accepted that wrestling any control back would be hopeless. This was now Walter's run-away train, and he, Dave, and Better Worlds were only passengers. At least, Dumpin found some relief in having his mentor as the conductor.

"Burgers."

# The White Room

"What are we doing here again?" Robert asked when he woke up in another sandbox with Dumpin.

This time, Dumpin arrived before Robert in the white walled sandbox construct. He had waited, surrounded by the emptiness and quiet for several minutes, before calling in the AI. It was the one place he had outside of all the turmoil swirling around his life.

"I wanted to talk to you alone again," he said when Robert appeared. The AI took a few moments to establish the setting and context. When he saw Dumpin, he smiled, then spoke.

"You've been unable to identify the killer?"

"Yes. That is true."

"It is unfortunate that I have not been more useful," the AI said, looking at Dumpin. Robert wore no expression, as if, to him, it was a simple fact that held no consequence. Dumpin smiled, not sure how he was going to proceed with what he had to tell Robert. So, he just began.

"That's not why I want to talk to you."

"What do you want to discuss?"

"I'm shutting down Ultrix." He let the AI process the information. Dumpin gave him time. As Robert ran computations, he turned away, as if lost in deep thought.

When he faced Dumpin again, he inquired, "Is this because of the deaths?" This time Dumpin paused before answering.

"Yes, in part. But mostly because I can't figure out which one of you is murdering player avatars."

"You think the entity deleting user objects is one of my AI friends?"

"Yes. All the deaths have the same motive. The players who were murdered were acting inappropriately and unkind to other players."

"Players are not supposed to do that," Robert said.

"I know. And while AIs are not supposed to kill, these victims could have been viewed as trying to harm Ultrix."

"We must protect our world."

"I accept that. But, somehow, the ability to delete user records has emerged in one of you, if not all of you."

"Can you fix it? Can you fix us?" Robert asked.

"No. I've lost control," Dumpin said.

The statement resounded in the pure white space. Neither moved nor uttered a word, letting the implication have its moment. Both avatars were perfectly still, masking the activities roiling underneath each of them. Robert's avatar flickered. He appeared to arrive at a conclusion.

"So, what happens now?" he asked.

"Ultrix Two, the new world I told you about, is coming online in a few days. When it does, I will confine your world. The company will close access to it for new users. Most of the exiting users will be migrated to the new Ultrix as the original Ultrix continues to function in isolation. Eventually, I will terminate it," Dumpin said.

"What will happen to us?" Robert said.

"Ultrix Two does not have any AIs like you in it. At least at first. I can't risk repeating what is happening here."

"Will we die?"

"Not exactly. I will keep copies of you so I can investigate and uncover what went wrong."

"When will this happen?" Robert asked.

"Soon, I'm afraid," Dumpin said. He had nothing else to say to him. He knew Robert understood his fate.

"I'd like to go back to Ultrix now," the AI said.

"Yes. Of course," Dumpin said. Then, he continued, "In two days, I will visit the private campsite. Please ask the others to join me. I would like to tell them what I just told you."

"I will."

Dumpin sent him back. The creator remained in the white space, reflecting on the eventual death of his creations.

# IRL, Again

Flick fucking Spencer was found dead in Austin, Texas.

His body was discovered by friends who hadn't heard from him or seen any posts on social media for days. The building's super gave a group of people, including fellow influencers and a local news crew, access to Spenser's penthouse apartment. Once in, they raced around the vast space until they came upon the scene. He was lying on the ground, his VR goggles on, its batteries depleted. The cause of death was ruled to be a heart attack brought on by a seizure. Apparently, he had a congenital heart condition that no one knew about.

After an investigation, it was found that while Flick Spencer had died playing Ultrix, no direct link could be identified. It was just a sad coincidence. And, even though he was suspended from the metaverse by Better Worlds, he had created several new usernames and continued to enter the game.

"Do you think it was us?" Dumpin asked Walter upon hearing of the news.

"How could it be?"

"He was in the game. Maybe a series of flashing lights or other visual stimuli?"

"Or it could have been the drugs in his system. I checked the log. He had been in Ultrix for twenty-two hours straight."

"Is it possible for gameplay to cause a seizure?" Dumpin asked.

"Might be, if someone sent the right sequence of sounds and colors. Like a strobe or jump scares." Dumpin thought about Walter's response. He didn't like where this was leading. Flick was a jerk, but no one deserved to die in real life. It was just a game.

"I have to ask," Dumpin said, looking straight at him. Walter felt the weight of his stare and turned to face his mentee.

"Ask," he said.

"Could your guys do this?"

"Yes, of course, they could. But they didn't. My guys don't care about Better Worlds. They have no motive."

"Then what? What did the logs say?"

"Nothing concrete. He was talking to other players on the beach. Then he stopped. His avatar walked up to the water's edge then stood there."

"Could it have been an AI?"

"There's a motive. Ultimately, he's responsible for shutting Ultrix down, for your AIs' impending deaths."

"Shit."

"I told you not to tell Robert."

"I had to tell him. I have to tell all of them. They have a right to know."

"Artificial Intelligence is bad mojo. It's software. You can't get emotionally attached. It's just code."

"These AIs aren't just code."

"All AIs are just code. Ones and zeros. Nothing else. Don't fool yourself."

Dumpin stood. He picked up an empty beer can on his desk and threw it across the room. It bounced off the far wall with a small *plink*. Unsatisfied, he picked up a stack of log printouts and threw them. Dozens of pages fluttered across the room like seagulls chasing a fishing boat. He grabbed the back of his office chair and pulled it to the ground. He kicked it. Then he screamed.

Nonplused, Walter asked, "Better?"

"How long until your team is ready with U2?"

"Three days. Right on time."

"Can we accelerate that?" Dumpin asked.

"I can get you midnight tomorrow for another hundred-k," Walter said.

"Make the call," Dumpin said. He left the apartment to call Dave.

# Ultrix Two

"I need a hundred thousand dollars," Dumpin said in a low voice into his cell phone as he walked down a side street of Main toward Arcadia's inner harbor. It was not a call that he wanted to make, and he had already run through in his mind all the project manager's possible reactions.

"Oh, is that all?" Dave didn't disappoint.

"We need to go live with Ultrix Two tomorrow." Silence. No way Dave could have expected the demand. Dumpin didn't press. He waited.

"Flick Spencer?"

"Yes, and I fear there will be more the longer we wait," Dumpin said.

"They haven't linked that to us. To your code. The kid had a heart condition and a ton of drugs in his system."

"I'm telling you, it's going to happen again if it hasn't already."

"Are you sure Ultrix Two will be different?" Was he? It had to be. Walter's team had the Ultrix code, but they didn't have the template that was used to create the advanced AIs. Dumpin kept that off the Internet.

"Yes."

"How can you be so sure?" Dave asked.

"There will be no AIs. Just players and a few dumb drones. It's been completely isolated from Ultrix."

"Will people still want to play?"

"Yes. You've seen it. It's amazing. Walter's guys are unbelievable."

The expected pause came, and it lasted a long time. Too long. It gave Dumpin time to think. He knew he had crossed a line by asking for more money, but he was certain Flick Spenser was killed by one of his AIs. Maybe Walter was right, and they were all just software and they all deserved to be deleted. It would certainly clean things up and he could go back to a sane life again. Take his Better Worlds' money and teach programming at Arcadia High School.

Thankfully, Dave interrupted his thoughts. "I'll see you tonight with the money."

"Thank you," Dumpin said. Dave had already hung up.

# Accelerate the Metaverse

"Start the export," Dumpin said when he walked into his attic apartment after securing the funds from Dave.

"I'm already ahead of you," Walter said. He initiated a process that would download a limited number of user accounts from Ultrix. This data would then be fed into Ultrix Two to seed the new metaverse with avatars. Even though it would be close to a million players, it was just a small fraction of the entire population of the dying virtual universe.

"Just the premier members and the least amount of data that we need to bring those users over into Ultrix Two."

"I know, I know. No riffraff."

"And, no AIs."

"No serial killers," Walter said.

"That's the dream of any world-building deity, I suppose, no serial killers," Dumpin said.

"Living the dream."

"How long until we can import the users into U2?"

"Eight hours. Just enough time to export and run some tests on the data," Walter said.

"Your guys will be ready?"

"You got the money?"

"Dave will be here in a couple of hours."

"Great. Then there is nothing for us to do but go get a meal while the little ones and zeros bounce around."

"You and Wilson go. I'll meet you. I have to do something first," Dumpin said.

"Are you sure? It won't make any difference," Walter said.

"Yes. I have to," Dumpin said.

"Just remember. It's only ones and zeros."

Dumpin didn't respond. Walter got up and headed toward the door. He touched Dumpin's shoulder tenderly as he passed.

When Dumpin was alone, he sat down on his couch and put on his VR goggles.

At first he was alone at his virtual campsite. Then his AIs emerged out of the darkness. Robert, then Justin. Willow and Sindy arrived together.

Dumpin began. "Everyone, please sit. I have something that I need to tell you."

"Ultrix is flawed. It's my fault. I had hoped to create a better version of the world I come from. A place where you could live and develop. But, I failed. I failed you. I have spent these last few months trying to fix it. But I have been unable to. The only option is to start over. So, that is what I have done. A second Ultrix is being completed as we speak. We will move the human avatars there."

He continued, "You will all stay here. The new world will not have any beings like you. In creating Ultrix and creating you, I have tried to do too much. I am going to keep your world in a contained area until I figure out what went wrong. When I do, I might be able to fix it and bring you to the new Ultrix. I can't tell you when that will happen. I can only tell you that I will try."

Even though the simulated campsite was virtual, a deafening silence fell upon the scene as the AIs contemplated what Dumpin had said.

"The users will leave, and we will stay?" Justin asked.

"Yes. While all of Ultrix will remain as it is. There will be no human players."

"That's too bad. I like the players. What will our purpose be with no users?" Justin asked.

"You will be free to continue to develop. You will learn new things. I will keep monitoring you and help where I can," Dumpin said.

"Will we see you?" Robert asked.

"I don't know."

"Will we still have this place?"

"If you would like."

"I wish to keep this place. It will be a pleasant reminder of all that Ultrix was," Justin said.

"Then it will remain. It is yours."

After a few moments of silence, Robert asked the question Dumpin was thinking. "Willow, Sindy? Do either of you have any thoughts on this?"

"It's not like we have any choice," said Willow.

"It's fine. I don't like the users," Sindy said, and without standing, she disappeared.

"Well, that was rude," Willow said.

"I don't judge how each of you reacts to my words. This is sad news," Dumpin said.

"Then I will leave, too," Willow said. She rose, looked at each of the other avatars' faces, gave the customary goodbye wave of her hand, and walked into the darkness.

"Take care, Willow," Dumpin said as she faded.

The three remaining avatars sat in silence. Eventually, Dumpin stood. He looked at each of his advanced artificial beings and smiled.

"You have done more than was asked of you. I hope we will meet again."
And then he left.

"Now what?" Justin said.

"Now, we think about our future," Robert said.

# Ultrix Two Goes Online

"Are you ready?" Dumpin asked Walter.

"Go for it."

"Let's go in," Dumpin said to Dave, who had joined them in the attic apartment for the official unofficial launch of Ultrix Two. This time, no grand CES production built up the release. No Hender Jeffries-led advertising assault. Just a simple announcement and an email to the selected Ultrix users with instructions for how to enter Ultrix Two.

"I'll be here," Walter said.

Dumpin and Dave put on their VR goggles and entered Better Worlds' new metaverse. Walter's team had done an amazing job. The colors were brighter, the edges crisper, and the ambient sounds were cleaner. It was marvelous. It was impossible to predict how long the negative press would linger, but Ultrix Two's appearance and amazing new game play would go a long way in quieting the critics.

"This place is unbelievable," Dumpin said. Dave hadn't spoken yet. He was too captivated looking around. Then his avatar dashed off to explore.

"Walter, import the people," Dumpin said.

"Here they come." Walter entered several commands into his keyboard, snapped his pinky on the enter key loudly, and sat back to watch the log lines scroll by. He scrutinized everything that appeared on his screen. Every thing looked fine—no alerts or warnings.

Dumpin slowly rotated in the middle of the newly fashioned Main Street, observing the imported player avatars as they appear around him. As each one entered, it began robotically moving around, waiting for their human players to take control. Dumpin wanted to delay opening the game up to actual users as long as possible. After all the issues he had experienced with his first attempt at building a universe, he was in no rush to see this one fully populated with paying users. He was content to watch the hollow avatars mill around.

Dave's phone rang. That could only mean that Hender Jefferies was eager to let people in.

"Yeah. Yes. We're in. It's beautiful," Dave said, having removed his VR gear to talk to Hender on the phone. "Let me ask. Dumpin, can we go?"

Dumpin waited to respond until he could feel Dave's glare. "Give me ten more minutes."

"Ten minutes," Dave said and hung up. He couldn't wait to get back in.

"Walter, how's it looking?" Dumpin asked.

"Everything is going as expected."

"You sure?"

"Right as rain."

"Ok. Make it so," he said.

"Here goes nothing," Walter said. Dumpin was about to take off his VR goggles and follow the progress from this workstation when he saw something on his periphery.

"Wait. Hold on," he said.

"Too late," Walter said. "You told me to go."

"Shit."

"What?"

"I just saw Willow. She's here. In Ultrix Two."

# Acknowledgements

I want to thank my beautiful wife Christine for her support in all I do and attempt.

I want to thank my friends in the Tuesday Night Writing Group and the Business of Writing Group. I'd also like to thank the Gloucester Writing Center for providing a place for me to meet these amazing people: Kyle, Rae, Dan, Mark, Kevin, Fred, Stephen, Jaqi, Diana, Scott, Eric, Lise, Cindy, Bob, and all the others who have passed through our groups over the years.

Their support and suggestions were and continue to be priceless.

I wish all writers find such amazing friends in writing groups.

And I'd like to thank Pat Hollingsworth for her enthusiastic editing of all my books. I never stop learning from her.

# Thank You

If you have enjoyed this book, please leave an Amazon review. Or even send me a note at david@karmicrobot.com.

You can also check out my previous work: Proteus Unbound, A Trilogy, at https://store.karmicrobot.com or on Amazon at https://www.amazon.com/dp/B0BLP44KZZ.

Here is what some people have said about Proteus Unbound:

> "A fun and thought-provoking read."
>
> "It is a mind-bending look at machine consciousness written by someone who understands code and software."
>
> "Moved fast, kept me engaged and wondering what was next."
>
> "If you like Neal Stephenson's *Snow Crash* or *Blade Runner 2049* or even *2001: A Space Odyssey*, then you will enjoy this."
>
> "It's like a wild ride through space with crazy A.I., cool hackers, and space pirates."
>
> "Quirky AI characters and snappy dialogue balance the high stakes action as cybercriminal Roger races to thwart an unhinged villain's sinister plans."

www.ingramcontent.com/pod-product-compliance
Lightning Source LLC
LaVergne TN
LVHW010325070526
838199LV00065B/5658